# NZ BOOK MONTH 2007

# THE SIX PACK TWO

## WINNING WRITING FROM NEW ZEALAND BOOK MONTH

First published in 2007 by New Zealand Book Month
with Whitireia Publishing

New Zealand Book Month
PO Box 52-016
Kingsland
Auckland 1352

ISBN: 978-1-877192-32-6

Production management and typesetting by
Hannah Bennett & Harriet Elworthy, Whitireia Publishing
Production supervision by Rachel Lawson
Cover design by Neil Pardington, Base Two
Printed by Astra Print, Wellington

# NZ BOOK MONTH 2007

2 September – 30 September 2007
www.nzbookmonth.co.nz

Last year the tremendous response to *The Six Pack* proved that New Zealanders are keen to enjoy local writing. The book spent three months at the top of the Booksellers New Zealand Bestsellers List for local fiction and the authors were widely acclaimed. Thousands of copies were sold, and thousands more were donated to schools and libraries across the country. *The Six Pack* showed that New Zealand Book Month's mission to celebrate New Zealand books and authors was underway.

That mission continues this year with *The Six Pack Two*. We received hundreds of entries for the 2007 competition. Five of the stories here were selected by our panel of judges and the sixth was voted for by the New Zealand public. Each of them is a wonderful example of what's happening on notebook pages, computer screens and old-fashioned typewriters across the country.

New Zealand Book Month features events throughout the country celebrating the creativity of New Zealand writers and their books. Check out our website for details on events in your community, and ways to get involved.

New Zealand is home to brilliant writing talent, providing readers with everything from gripping thrillers to esoteric essays. Whatever your taste, there is a fantastic New Zealand book for you. We hope that New Zealand Book Month introduces you to some new favourite writers and prompts you to explore New Zealand's literary landscape.

# CONTENTS

# FOREWORD

Writers, like our artists, designers and musicians, are making the country a more exciting place, and redefining what it is to be a New Zealander in 2007.

Our writers and the books we publish are in great shape, whether it is international success like Lloyd Jones' prizewinning novel *Mister Pip*, or the exciting new works from emerging writers.

Last year's inaugural New Zealand Book Month was a great success. The first *Six Pack* sold well, making the New Zealand Fiction Bestsellers List for three months. With its fresh mix of new and established writers, it put New Zealand writing into the hands of a new audience.

The Labour-led Government has backed New Zealand Book Month because it is worth supporting. It is strongly endorsed by book publishers, booksellers and corporate sponsors, and it involves book lovers throughout the country.

The first New Zealand Book Month made a promising start. Many New Zealanders took part in the campaign to celebrate our books and writers. I hope many more take part in 2007.

Rt. Hon. Helen Clark
Prime Minister
Minister of Arts, Culture and Heritage
August 2007

# INTRODUCTION

The day before judging, I bumped into John Campbell, a judge for the first *Six Pack*, and told him that I had been passed the mantle he carried the year before. 'Oh, marvellous,' he boomed, before imparting conspiratorially, 'but really, Miriama, how on earth they expect five judges of different backgrounds and firm opinion to come to a consensus . . . I mean, last year, it was a bloody nightmare!' Well, this year was quite different. Where John and his panel debated wildly, the judging panel for *The Six Pack Two* agreed quite amiably on almost every selection. There couldn't have been a clearer demonstration to me that the practice of judging, reviewing or critiquing literature can invite quite different responses, that consensus of opinion is really a very arbitrary thing.

It is, I suppose, the frustration (and joy) of any writer at review time. In *The Envoy from Mirror City*, Janet Frame describes the confusion of receiving conflicting reviews for *Scented Gardens for the Blind*: one said 'This book is unreadable in the worst sense,' and another described it as 'likely a work of genius.'

So I had mentally prepared to stand by my 'unreadables' and debate the 'genius' selections of my fellow judges. I went away from my meeting with John feeling mildly excited, and a little terrified, about the notion of going head-to-head with Dame Fiona Kidman, Finlay MacDonald, Joan Mackenzie and Elizabeth Caffin. I resolved that I would stand defiantly by my opinion in the face of greater experience and credentials. After all, I saw myself as a representative of one of the judging criteria: 'It must have broad appeal.' (I'm not sure whether I compliment or damn myself with that thought.)

But I was robbed of the chance to expostulate grandly. We rarely disagreed. If concerns such as genre balance distracted us, we returned to the bottom line for judging *The Six Pack Two*: the quality of the writing. By dint of being good writing, we felt our choices achieved the aim of 'broad appeal'. And I must admit, I was somewhat relieved, and not a little smug, to discover that my opinions were shared by some of the country's literary lights. But how did we reach consensus so easily? Was it luck that we five all agreed on the selection? Was it that the pieces we chose clearly stood out above the others? Or was it proof of John's assertion in his introduction last year that literary competitions are 'about as rational as a meteor shower'? It may have been a mix of all these factors.

For me the selection came down to this: 'Kathy and Tim'

is simple and elegant, and who can't, in some way, relate to the dramas of dating? I loved the sweet, tragic innocence of 'Scout's Honour': '"Bog girl," hot peanut-butter-breath sang in my face.' There was 'The Yard Broom', dark, bleak and edgy: 'They were Nathan's cousins but I was afraid of them,' and the social satire of 'Foodbanquet': 'you couldn't own a McCahon and not display it.' Then the furious, raw grief of 'Note Left on a Window', a piece marked by its unrelenting and often merciless observations: 'She thought she could talk to me, that I would stand and listen to her melodic blabbing, the cadence of a born slag.' And then there was the perfect rendering of high school politics in 'In the Back of a VW', which overflows with delightful jealousies and youthful idealism. Readers clearly agreed, choosing it as their favourite in the online poll.

What the judging panel often debated was the consistency of excellence throughout any given piece. A lovely turn of phrase for one judge might well be an irritation for another. But I felt all the pieces we selected showed unapologetic and honest storytelling. These are pieces crafted to withstand the criticism of others after being pushed out from the safe haven of their authors. They are stories imbued with the writer's sense of self-belief; a quality Janet Frame, despite all her insecurities, obviously had in spades. When receiving conflicting reviews, she retreated to an excellent stronghold, one that would serve any writer well:

> This confusing experience reminded me of what I already knew, and strengthened my resolution never to forget that a writer must stand on the rock of her self and her judgment or be swept away by the tide or sink in the quaking earth: there must be an inviolate place where the

choices and decisions, however imperfect, are the writer's own, where the decision must be as individual and solitary as birth or death.

*The Envoy from Mirror City*

*The Six Pack Two* represents our consensus; it is essentially a guide to what *we* feel is quality New Zealand storytelling. If your opinion is different from ours, then so be it. You, the reader, have had the opportunity to read all fifteen shortlisted pieces on the New Zealand Book Month website, and to judge for yourself. And in that most magnificent tradition of readers, writers and critics, you may disagree with our selection. That is the wonderful thing about the literary world: the absence of any correct answer, the potential for great debate and the often fruitless hope for eventual consensus.

I love New Zealand writing. Since I first picked up Witi Ihimaera's *Pounamu Pounamu* as a child, and went on to discover Keri Hulme, Maurice Gee, Margaret Mahy, Frank Sargeson, Katherine Mansfield, the inimitable Janet Frame, oh and so many more, I have displayed their books in my collection as shameless testament to my 'obvious excellent taste' in literature.

I am pleased to present this collection and proud to have been part of a process that gives six New Zealand writers this platform to show off their work. New Zealand Book Month honours our writing community, which includes and welcomes the authors featured in *The Six Pack Two*. But New Zealand Book Month is not just about writers. In reading, enjoying and discussing the stories in this book, you too play a role in New Zealand literature.

Miriama Kamo

# FAITH OXENBRIDGE

Faith Oxenbridge has spent most of her life in Christchurch, with short stints in Auckland, Sydney, London and Israel. She grew up in a semi-rural area and spent most of her adolescence trying to get lifts into town, where the action was. She now lives in town and dreams of living in a semi-rural area. She has been a teacher, bookseller, café owner and sheep dagger, and still is a mother. She currently works for the Christchurch Arts Festival, writes theatre reviews for the *Listener* and is completing a Master of Fine Arts in Creative Writing at the University of Canterbury. 'In the Back of a VW' is from a collection of stories for her MFA, titled *The Not Quite Right Club*.

# IN THE BACK OF A VW

Rima is the only girl in the seventh form – apart from the Christians and brainy girls – who hasn't had sex. She could have done it in the car with Pete Neilson after the sixth form dance if she'd allowed things to progress past the vigorous pashing he inflicted on her in his Hillman Imp at the bottom of her shingle drive, and again last Saturday with a St Bede's boy who groped her at a party on Cashmere Hill. But so far all these experiences have left Rima cold. One minute she is at a party talking to seemingly nice boys and the next they're lunging at her, thrusting their beery tongues into her mouth as if they have lost something in there. At these parties nearly everyone ends up on a couch or in a corner pashing and those who don't are left swaying stupidly in the middle of the room to *Dark Side of the Moon* trying to pretend that they are having a good time.

Rima's best friend Wendy is never left dancing in the middle of the room. Having Wendy as a best friend has been both a blessing and a curse. Wendy is the prettiest girl in the seventh form. She wins the school athletics cup every year, has perfect legs – apart from a wart on her knee that should look disgusting but on her looks cute – golden skin that tans under a light bulb, and she is unnaturally nice and kind-hearted. She is nice to the Christians and the brainy girls – who Rima avoids for fear of being claimed as one of their own. She is nice to the spotty chess club and orchestra boys who send her wistful glances and notes in class, and is even nice to the daggy teachers with bad breath and dandruff who pretty much everyone else despises.

Wendy and Rima have been best friends since the first day of the third form when Wendy rescued Rima from her lonely bench by the gymnasium by asking her if she wanted to sit with her group at lunch. Things could have been different. Rima was wearing the wrong shoes – roman sandals instead of T-bars – and the wrong hair – plaits instead of loose bunches – but Wendy was too nice to notice her fashion faux pas or the fact that she had a plate and stick insect legs. Rima still wonders how they became friends. Wendy is relentlessly normal. She doesn't spend hours in front of the bathroom mirror worrying about whether her boobs will grow, and she doesn't lie awake at night praying that some David Cassidy lookalike will skate with her at the Centauris Rink on a Saturday afternoon and that if he does her hand won't sweat so much that he accidentally-on-purpose lets go of it after only one lap. Even Wendy's periods are normal. Rima haemorrhages for eight abnormal days and waddles around school with several super-size pads sandwiched soggily between her legs, while Wendy drips delicately into a single regular pad for four regular days each month.

Wendy's parents are normal too. When Rima stays the night, Wendy's mother gets up early and cooks them pancakes in a frilly pinny. Her father has a men's apparel shop and wears black slacks and shirts with collars even in the weekend. At the dinner table everyone is polite and Wendy's mother is up and down getting drinks and food as if it's what she really loves to do. They say grace – without giggling – before dinner and no one shouts, argues, punches, picks their teeth, burps, moans about the food, or tries to steal the meat off their neighbour's plate when they're not looking.

Wendy had sex in the sixth form with Shane Tobin, a surfing-mad seventh former with long, sea-bleached hair, who nearly every girl in the senior school was in love with. Before Shane Tobin, Wendy and Rima had a pact that they wouldn't have sex until they were nineteen, and that they would try and have it at the same time so that neither of them was left out. When Wendy told her she had done it, Rima felt the same as when her cat, Bob, was run over by Mr Sullivan's tractor and she found his mangled body in the paddock next door. Shane Tobin eventually dumped Wendy to get back with the girlfriend he'd had before her who surfed and smoked pot. Shane told Wendy that sex with girls who smoked pot was way better because it drove them wild. Wendy refused to smoke pot with Shane, which Rima was relieved about because she has never smoked pot but mostly because it meant that Shane dumped Wendy and Rima could have her back, almost virginal again, but Wendy hasn't got over Shane and still carries a picture of him surfing at Taylors Mistake in her wallet.

When Rima turned fifteen her mother tried to have a sex talk with her. Her older sisters Jenny and Bea warned her that it was coming. Apparently her mother read somewhere that fifteen was the right age to talk to daughters about sex, but she must have read something that was written a hundred years ago because Rima has known about sex since she was ten like pretty much everyone else. The talk took place in Rima's bedroom and only lasted one minute.

'I'd like to have a talk with you about . . . about growing up and . . . sex,' her mother said, hovering wraith-like in the doorway. Rima had been waiting for this and was prepared.

'It's OK, Mum. I know all about it.'

'You haven't . . .'

'Of course not,' Rima said, blushing a little.

'Well if there's anything you want to know, please just ask,' her mother said and then drifted away.


Rima has had two mums. There was the strong, wise, laughing and loving mum she had from birth until she was eight, who is a precious yet increasingly vague memory. This was the mum who just had to look at Rima to know what she was thinking, and the mum who always knew the words to say to make anything bad all right again. Then there is the mum who went into hospital and came home a ghost. Jenny, who thinks she knows everything now that she has a boyfriend and is at teachers college, calls the second mum Zombie Mum. Rima has to share a bedroom with Jenny, which is hell. Rima's first mum would not have made her share a bedroom with Jenny because she would have known how hard it was. Jenny moans about everything. Dad calls her Moaning Minnie, and First

Mum used to say Jenny was born with a chip on her shoulder the size of Mt Cook. Zombie Mum hardly says anything. First Mum also used to say that Rima was a rose between thorns. The other thorn is Rima's oldest sister, Bea, who is at journalism school in Wellington.

In the seventh form the teachers treat you like human beings. Rima has a new English teacher called Carly, like Carly Simon. The class is allowed to call her Carly instead of Miss Mitchell, which is unheard of at Rima's school. Carly says that 'Miss' is a label she can do without anyway, thank you very much. Carly is twenty-three, wears batik skirts down to the ground and necklaces she makes herself out of dyed haricot beans, and is a feminist. Wendy says that means she probably doesn't shave her legs or wear Mum antiperspirant, and when Rima told her parents that her English teacher was a feminist, her father rolled his eyes spastically and said, 'Lord save me.' Bea was down for the university break at the time and threw a mental.

'What do you mean, Brian?' Bea said dangerously. Now that she was an adult and almost a journalist, Bea had taken to calling her parents Brian and Angela.

'Bloody feminists,' he said, shaking his head, either oblivious to or uncaring of Bea's about-to-boil-over rage, 'they're women who just want to become men.'

'We don't want to become men, actually, Brian.' Bea spat out her father's name as if it were a piece of rotten apple. 'We just want equality. Marilyn Waring came to talk to us last term and said that more and more women are attending university and that the National Party are going to implement policies to encourage more women to apply for management positions.'

'Marilyn Waring is a twit,' he yelled. 'Don't mention

that woman's name in this house. It's bad enough that we have to listen to a woman reading the news now, but at least she looks like a woman. If you support that she-devil and Piggy Muldoon, Beatrice, then you're no daughter of mine.'

'You're the pig,' Bea yelled back. 'A male chauvinist pig!'

For their novel study this year, Carly is going to get the school to buy a class set of a book by an English author called Margaret Drabble. She told the class that she had a bit of a run-in with the Head of English, Mr Pritchard, who wears walk socks and speaks like a BBC announcer. He said that the set novel for the seventh form was *Oliver Twist* by Charles Dickens, and Carly said, 'I think they need to read something a little more relevant to their lives,' which made Mr Pritchard's neck go instantly red and blotchy. Carly asked the class if anyone had heard of Margaret Drabble and only Natasha Carter, who has bad skin and a mother who's a university lecturer, put her hand up. Rima wanted to put her hand up. She badly wanted to have heard of Margaret Drabble. First Mum used to read all the time and has the whole set of Shakespeare's plays and poetry, but Zombie Mum has trouble concentrating. Zombie Mum reads romances. Rima is a very good English student and last year won a competition for a story she wrote about summer holidays on Banks Peninsula, but she has never heard of Margaret Drabble.

Wendy is bored with school and wants to apply to be an air hostess. She read in a magazine that the most important attributes you need to be an air hostess are impeccable grooming and a welcoming smile, and thinks this sounds just like her. Rima feels like she has been punched in the stomach.

'Don't you want to get Bursary and keep your options open? You might change your mind.'

'I don't think so. I've always wanted to be an air hostess.'

'I thought you wanted to be a kindergarten teacher? You love kids,' Rima says, somewhere between pleading and persuasion.

'I do, but Mum and Dad said this would be a better career choice and I agree.'

'But an air hostess is just a waitress in a uniform.'

'That's not quite true,' Wendy says calmly. 'You learn First Aid, Grooming, and how to keep your head in an emergency.' Wendy can't see the point of being in the seventh form now that she knows what she wants to do and her father says she would be better off learning practical skills like shorthand and typing, and Shane Tobin is no longer at school, or even in Christchurch. His father made him join the army because he was smoking too much pot.


Carly has been reading the class some poems by a New Zealand poet called James K Baxter. The only poetry Rima has heard up to now has been poetry she couldn't – and didn't want to – understand, about God and flowers and boring crap. Carly says that Baxter's poems are about people who live on the margins of our society and that they help us understand that life is complex and often inexplicable. When Carly reads the poems in her sing-song voice, Rima's chest feels tight, as if she has just seen a boy she likes across the room at a party. Even the boys are quiet when she recites, although this could be because they think she is a hot chick and Jeff McDowell, the class creep, says he reckons she'd go off with a bang.

Rima hears Mark Rehu, a new Maori boy from the North Island, ask Carly after class if she knows of any good Maori poets he can read. Carly says he should read Hone Somebody and that she will bring a book of his poems from home for him tomorrow. Rima has had a thing for Mark Rehu ever since he chose her as his partner for ballroom dancing in PE and Wendy said that must mean he likes her. Wendy also said that he seems very nice and well mannered for a Maori. There are only a few Maoris at their school and they are nearly all in detention every night. Bea says that's because New Zealanders like to pretend they aren't racist but that racism is institutionalised in our country and that really we aren't much better than South Africa. Rima's father says he doesn't know what Bea is going on about and that he doesn't give a rat's arse about the colour of a bloke's skin. His best friend is a Maori called Bill Hohepa who he met on a shearing gang, but Wendy's mother wouldn't let her go out with a boy from Aranui High in the fifth form because he was a Maori.

There is something mysterious about Mark. Rima has been reading her mother's romances and Mark reminds her of the men — some of them are Italian or Greek, so a Maori hero is feasible — who don't say a lot but look intense and inscrutable. In the romances no one has sex or pashes. Instead, there are long, burning looks and lots of jaw tensing and right at the end before they declare their love for each other there is a kiss that never involves tongues or saliva. That's what Rima wants.

'How's the groovy new English teacher?' Rima's dad asks at the dinner table, wriggling his bushy eyebrows like an idiot.

'Good,' Rima says coolly. She doesn't want to talk to her parents about Carly and the poetry and how it makes her feel. She doesn't want to talk to them about anything important that happens in her life. How could she? In the books she reads, girls ask their mothers about sex and whether they should 'go' with a boy, but in real life no one does that. Her father makes jokes about everything, which was fine when she was seven, but now that she's seventeen, it's not. Haven't her parents noticed that she is no longer a child? Lately she has been thinking about how good it will be when she leaves home.

'Bit of a cool chick is she?' Rima's dad says, unable to let go of the joke that wasn't even funny in the first place.

'Brian!' Zombie Mum says, clicking out of her coma for a moment.

'What?' he says. 'Aren't I allowed to say "chick"? Am I too old to know what's cool?'

'Yes, actually,' Rima says, finishing her meal and standing to leave the table, 'you are too old to know what's cool. In fact you're too old to even use the word "cool".' Rima can hear her dad and Jenny laughing as she leaves the room, but she doesn't care. She's sick of being the rose between thorns. She wants to be a thorn for a while and someone else can be the rose. When Bea left home Rima was excited. Bea has opinions on everything and never shuts up and Rima imagined that with Bea gone there would be more space for her, but now there is too much space. Rima realises that Bea's constant prattle covered up Jenny's moaning, her father's lame jokes and her mother's zombie silence.

Rima goes into the lounge and puts Neil Young's *Harvest* on the turntable. Bea has left her albums behind, but with strict instructions that none of her sisters are to play them. Any minute now, Jenny will open the door and say, 'I'm telling Bea on you.' Rima has two albums of her own that she saved for with her babysitting money: Elton John's *Goodbye Yellow Brick Road* and *The Best of Bread*. If she has a bad day or her period is due, she plays *The Best of Bread* and cries. The songs that make her cry the most are the ones about love that goes wrong or love that can never be. Recently she has started playing Bea's albums, and in particular Neil Young and Bob Dylan, because Carly gave them some Bob Dylan lyrics to study as poetry and says that Bob Dylan is one of the world's greatest living poets. Rima is trying to like Bob Dylan, even though he sounds like one of the deranged animals on *Sesame Street*.

When Rima listens to music everything seems both sad and beautiful at the same time. She thinks about Mark and how wonderful it will be when they fall in love. She imagines them reading poetry together and exchanging burning looks. She thinks about Carly and whether she is brave enough to ever become a feminist. She thinks about how she needs to get having sex out of the way so that she can say she's done it. Wendy says it isn't as bad as you think it's going to be and mostly it's over and done with really quickly. Wendy has only ever had sex in the back of Shane's VW, and says that her years of doing gym helped because there wasn't a lot of room, especially when his surfboard was there. On her fifteenth-birthday sex talk, Rima was dismissive to her mother and said there was nothing she needed to know, but there are many things she would like to know. She would like to know what it means if you find pashing boring. She would like to know if it's true that a boy might put his dick in your mouth, and what you are supposed to do if he does. And what happens to the stuff that comes out of you when you've done it? Are you supposed to get up and wipe it off straight away or do you just pretend that it's not there?

The Margaret Drabble book is about a girl from a posh family in England who is at university and gets pregnant.

Carly says it is a coming of age novel, and when some of the boys complain that it's a girls' book, she says it will be good for them to understand how it is to be a woman and that for too long literature has been dominated by the male voice. The rugby boys, who are only at school for the First Fifteen and already have their trade apprenticeships lined up for next year, laugh when Carly says 'coming of age', because of the 'coming'. Carly gives them a withering look and tells them to grow up.

The novel pulls Rima deep into its strange yet familiar world. When she finishes, she feels as if she has woken up from a dream or been to a movie during the day and coming out into the light is almost unbearable. She wants more. Carly gives her a book called *Catcher in the Rye,* by an American writer, and tells Rima that it's students like her that make her job worthwhile.

Rima bikes home from school with wings. It's good that she has the new book and Carly's praise to distract her, because things are not good at home. Her mother is going down. Every so often her mother goes down, not as badly as the first time when she spent three months in hospital having the electric shock treatment that turned her into a zombie, but bad enough. Going down means that Rima's mother stays in bed for weeks. Everything goes down when Rima's mother goes down. Her father stops making jokes and wears a permanent frown and the house feels cold and grey, and so does Rima.

Rima's mother and father go to see the psychiatrist who her father says is a Yank who wears a dress. Her mother almost smiles and says, 'It's a kaftan, not a dress.' The psychiatrist gives Rima's mum some new pills and her husband keeps them locked in a cupboard and hands them out to her every night. Atavan, Amoxapine and Trazodone. They sound like flesh-ripping dinosaurs but look like lollies.

Wendy has put in an application for air hostess training and finds out in a month. Shane Tobin has written to her from army camp in Waiouru in the North Island. She carries his letter with her everywhere.

*Dear Wens*
*The Army stinks. The Officers are wankers and there is*
*no sea for miles. It's freezing at night but the food is OK.*
*Dad says if I stick the year out, I can come home and do an*
*apprenticeship as a fitter and turner, so I'm sticking it out.*
*Did you know I broke up with Paula? She was a spinner.*
*I miss you and think about you heaps. Do you have a*
*boyfriend? Do you still have that wart on your knee? I'm*
*coming down in August for a week and was wondering if*
*you'd like to go for a drive or something?*
*Shane x*

Wendy is over the moon and says that if Shane asked her to marry him she'd say yes. Rima tells Wendy she could do way better than Shane.

'He's not good enough for you. All he cares about is surfing and sex.'

Wendy fiddles with the wart on her knee, like she always does when she is upset.

'You know, Rima,' she says quietly to her wart, 'you're getting really up yourself this year.' The worst thing you can be at school is 'up yourself'. Rima's sister Bea was 'up herself' and no one liked her much. She had to go to her Leavers Ball on her own – which she said she didn't give a stuff about – because no boy wanted to take her.

'I am not up myself,' Rima says indignantly, 'I just think there is more to life than falling in love and thinking about getting married. There's a whole world of experiences and adventures out there waiting for us. Carly says we are part of a silent revolution and that we need to forge new paths for ourselves.'

'I'm happy with just falling in love and getting married actually,' Wendy says, 'and if you want to go and fight in a revolution then you'll have to do it without me. I'm not like you, Rima.'

Carly puts Rima into a group with Mark Rehu and Natasha Carter to analyse the central character's journey from adolescent to adult in Margaret Drabble's novel. They are to present it as a wallchart and graph the elements that make her change. Wendy is put with a couple of the rugby boys but doesn't care and says the novel was boring and doesn't have enough story. She is waiting to hear from the airline for her real life to begin and if she doesn't get in she will leave school anyway and work in a chemist shop.

Rima's group goes to the library to do their project. Natasha Carter has been on medication for her acne and looks almost pretty.

'I think a pivotal point in the character's journey is when she has sex for the first time,' Natasha says. Rima is surprised that she can say sex without blushing. Maybe even Natasha Carter has had sex?

'Definitely,' Mark says, and Rima tries to think of something to say that will impress him more. She says she thinks finding out she is pregnant is equally pivotal, and Mark nods thoughtfully, but doesn't say definitely. Natasha frowns.

'I don't know,' she says, 'don't you think when she challenges her parents' expectations and decides to keep the baby is when she really comes of age?'

Rima was invited to Natasha's birthday party last year. She had no idea why and wasn't going to go but Wendy said it would be rude not to. There was only Rima, another (drippy) girl from school and a boy from Christ's College called Julian. Julian didn't look anything like the boys Rima knew from school. He wore a blue and white striped shirt and jeans with a crease ironed in them and spoke with the confidence of an adult. Natasha's mother cooked a fondue and let them each have a glass of red wine from France. There was orchestra music playing in the background and Natasha's mother asked them questions about their lives and what they hoped to do when they left school. Julian said he wanted to be a lawyer and Natasha said she was undecided. Rima had no idea what she wanted to do, but said she wanted to be a journalist so that she could tell the truth about things.

'Interesting,' Natasha's mother said. 'What would you like to tell the truth about, Rima?'

'Umm,' Rima said, trying to remember some of the things Bea used to rant on about, 'social injustices and stuff, I suppose.'

'Well there are plenty of those to expose,' Natasha's mother, who told them all to please call her Bronwyn, said emphatically.

'Definitely!' Rima said and tried to change the subject.

In the library, as Natasha speaks about the novel's underlying themes and how the central character's journey illuminates them, Rima is reminded of how she felt that night at Natasha's house. Rima is brainy; she's in the top stream – even though her reports always say she could do better – and her sister Bea was Dux of the school and is always going on about politics and stuff, but in Rima's house no one talks about anything much apart from what's for dinner and on the telly that night. Her parents don't drink alcohol and have a bottle of sherry in the china cabinet for when people come to visit, which is rare, and her mother cooks a different cut of meat from the freezer every night with veges from the garden and wouldn't even know what a fondue was. Sometimes Rima's dad will ask them at the dinner table what they learned at school that day or say something about how bloody Piggy Muldoon is ruining the country, and he cried last year when Norm Kirk died, even though he votes for Social Credit, but mostly they all just wolf their food down and then ask what's for pudding.

The new pills are not working and the kaftan-wearing psychiatrist, whose name is Harold Weinberg, says that Rima's mother might have to go back into hospital for more shock treatment, but she surprises everyone by saying she won't go. Then she shocks everyone more by saying she wants to try going off her drugs because she is sick of feeling like the walking dead. Rima's dad and Harold Weinberg advise her not to, but she is adamant. Rima is both alarmed and hopeful. If her mother becomes more mental she's not sure she will cope, but if there is even a small chance she can have her old mother back, then she is willing to believe. The psychiatrist says she has to cut back on her antidepressants slowly, one-eighth of a pill at a time, and monitor her reactions. Rima's mother cuts the corners off them at the kitchen table with her husband watching nervously over her shoulder.

There was a time when her mother's mentalness had Rima's gut churning like a concrete mixer day and night. There was a time also, a long time, when Rima thought if she was very good and helped around the house and did well at school and kept her room tidy and told her mother jokes and funny stories that she might get better. But she didn't and now Rima has discovered music and books, and has Carly and her dreams of Mark to stop her feeling sick every time her mother lies in bed all day crying, or makes her lean over the balcony and tell the Sunday visitors who pull up the drive in their Sunday best that her parents aren't home, even though their car is parked in the garage for all the world to see.

Natasha, Mark and Rima get an A for their assignment and Wendy gets into air hostess training. She has a party in her garage and Rima and Wendy get drunk on Cold Duck and start crying about how much they love each other and also Shane and Mark. Rima pashes Jeff McDowell and then chunders in Wendy's father's radishes. She discovers that pashing isn't so bad when you're drunk and might have even let Jeff go further if she hadn't spewed.

Mark isn't at the party even though he was invited along with the whole seventh form. Rima has never seen Mark at a party. He is a mystery. He has no friends and is nowhere to be seen at lunchtime at school when everyone else hangs out in the common room. The rugby boys say that Mark is probably a homo. Wendy says she thinks he is just shy and that Rima should come out and tell him how she feels.

Rima thinks he is shy too until she hears him reading the part of King Lear in English. She has to read the part of Cordelia, King Lear's youngest and most honest daughter, which she can relate to, being a reluctant rose between thorns.

If Rima wasn't truly in love with Mark before he reads the part of King Lear like an actor in a movie and gives her skin goose bumps, then she is now. Even Carly is moved by his performance and when she says, 'Thank you, Mark, that was truly inspiring,' and the rugby heads at the back of the class snigger, she loses it.

'What's so funny, meatheads?' Carly says nastily, going almost purple with anger. There is silence from the back and everyone else looks down at their battered copies of *King Lear*.

'You know, there is more to life than kicking a ball around and getting pissed, but I feel sorry for you guys because that is all you are ever going to know.' Then she stomps out of the room, almost tripping on her billowing batik skirt.

Now that Wendy has gone, Rima sits with Mark and Natasha in English and in the other classes too. They are becoming something of a threesome. Rima doesn't particularly want to be associated with Natasha because even though her skin has cleared up and she is washing her hair more, she is still a little weird. She is only there for Mark and has good Mark days, when he gives her a smile from the queue in the tuckshop, or asks her about her weekend or what she thought of a class. Then she is almost certain that he is in love with her too but is too shy to do anything about it. There are bad Mark days too, when he doesn't even seem to know that she is there; days when he is sullen and distracted. Then Rima consoles herself that he is morose because of his frustrated love for her.

At Carly's urging the three of them go and see a play at the Court Theatre called *The Birthday Party* by Harold Pinter. Rima has never been to the theatre before and even though the play makes no sense and doesn't seem to go anywhere or even finish properly, it seems to be telling her something profound. She doesn't know what it is but it flaps in her gut like a thousand trapped butterflies, or that could be because her knee is almost touching Mark's. Rima has sat next to Mark in class a hundred times, but never this close and in the dark. She has dreamed about sitting next to him like this. He is wearing Old Spice – for her? – and she has on Jenny's Jovan Musk, which Jenny would punch her for if she found out. It's worth the punch though and she hopes that Mark can smell it and that it will cast a spell on him as the ad in the *Seventeen* magazine promises. But Mark doesn't seem to know she is there and at half-time all he wants to talk about is the play. He says he can't wait to tell Carly about it. He says Carly told him to think less about the words the characters use and more about what lies beneath and between them.

'You mean the subtext,' Natasha says, sounding bored.

'Yes,' Mark says uncertainly.

In the car on the way home when Natasha's mother asks them what they thought of the play, both Mark and Rima can't think of anything to say. Natasha says it was both surreal and menacing. Natasha's mother nods her head vigorously and Rima decides in that moment that she is going to become the sort of person who uses words like surreal and menacing. Rima's head is spinning. The play and the books she has been reading have thrust her into a strange and exciting new world and even though she often feels like a disoriented day tripper, she is increasingly certain that it is where she belongs.

Rima's mother can't sleep. She is jittery and jumps at the slightest thing. She goes for long walks up the hill with her husband but is still on edge. Sometimes she can't eat her dinner because her hands shake so much. She is becoming a whole different sort of mother again. Instead of going to bed at eight and sleeping around the clock, she paces around Rima and Jenny's bedroom.

'Tell me about the play,' she fires at Rima the night she comes home from the Court Theatre.

'It was surreal,' Rima says without emotion. Her mother nods like an excited child, but Rima keeps her eyes on the page of her book, willing her strange mother to leave. She doesn't know if she can cope with another new mother.

'What are you reading?' she says.

'*The God Boy*,' Rima says.

'What's it about?'

'It's about a boy called Jimmy Sullivan who gets screwed up by his parents.'

'Would I like it?' Rima's mother asks like a five-year-old. Rima does not need a five-year-old mother at the moment. For years she bled for her mother and felt the weight of her misery as if it was her own. When she first came out of hospital and Bea overheard the doctors telling their father she was suicidal and should not be left alone, Rima followed her from room to room and would even wake in the night to check that she was asleep in bed and not lying in a river somewhere with stones in her pockets.

'Keep an eye on your mother, Rima,' her father would say every time he went out to the farm. He never said 'keep an eye' to Bea and Jenny, just Rima. At first it made her feel proud and special, but over the years Rima's spirit has been seeping out like a slow puncture.

'I don't know,' Rima says impatiently, and feels both relief and guilt when her mother leaves the room silently.

★

It's a long winter. The cold burns Rima's exposed knees as she bikes to school on the icy roads, but little else registers in her almost-always-elsewhere brain. She studies with Mark and Natasha in the library at lunchtimes, and at home only leaves her bedroom and books for meals. Her mother has cut her pills by a quarter and is bouncing off the walls. Her father is worried and has even considered slipping the missing quarter into her nightly Horlicks because at least when she stays all day in bed he knows where she is. Jenny spends more and more time at her boyfriend Neil's house so Rima almost has her own room. Bea writes brief, matter-of-fact letters from Wellington and says when she finishes she will become a foreign correspondent in a war zone.

Rima gets the second to top mark in the mock English Bursary exam. Natasha beats her by three marks and says 'well done' with such a superior tone that Rima wants to spew. Mark trips up in the poetry analysis section so Carly gives him private tuition at lunchtimes. Wendy rings most nights but it's getting hard to find things to talk about. She has been learning about what shade of lipstick suits her skin tone and how to care for her cuticles. Shane is coming back to Christchurch in a month and Wendy and her mother have started shopping for her glory box. Wendy's mother says it takes years of careful shopping to fill a glory box properly.

Rima finds Mark in the library one lunchtime without his nose in a book. He is staring vacantly out the window. Rima sits at his table and starts to talk about their *King Lear* essay but he doesn't respond.

'Are you OK?' Rima says. Mark turns and looks at her as if he has only just registered her presence.

'I suppose so,' he says. 'I've just got some things on my mind.'

'Do you want to talk about it?' Rima says, her heart

leaping. Me, she thinks, is it me on your mind?

'I would if I could,' Mark says, looking out the window again, 'but it's pretty complicated and I don't know if you could cope.'

'Try me,' Rima says, smiling in a way that she hopes will say, 'I love you too.' He looks at her. It is a long, burning look that sears her heart. She is on the verge of either fainting or declaring her love for him outright, when the bell goes.

'I've got Biology,' Mark mumbles and picks up his bag and leaves.

There's only a month to go until exams and Rima has two things to look forward to: beating Natasha Carter in the English Bursary exam and Carly's pre-exam class barbecue at her flat in town, where Rima is certain she and Mark are going to get together. They have barely spoken since the library incident, but now that Rima is sure of his feelings, she's in no hurry.

Rima's mother sets out for a walk in the hills behind the house one Saturday morning and doesn't come back. Rima and her father spend the whole afternoon walking through the windswept, gorse-ridden hills calling her name into a ferocious easterly. At four o'clock her father says, 'Jesus bloody Christ,' and drops to the ground as if he has been shot. He squats on his haunches and rocks and sobs. Rima puts her hand on his shuddering shoulder and tells him that it's all right, that she's probably just fallen asleep somewhere or is waiting for them at home right now, peeling the potatoes.

Rima is putting mutton chops in the oven when the police ring to say they have her mother at the Papanui Police Station. She'd walked over the hills and into town and had fallen asleep on a bench somewhere in Papanui until someone called the police. That night she is crazy-jolly and when Rima asks why she'd walked so far, she just says because she felt like it. Rima's father says enough is enough and the next day takes her back into hospital for assessment.

Carly's flat is a big old villa on the banks of the Avon. The lounge is decorated with posters of Che Guevara, John Lennon, and Wonder Woman, who Carly says is a feminist icon. Jeff McDowell asks if that's because her tits are so big and Carly doesn't laugh, so he mutters something about feminists having no sense of humour. There is incense burning and someone called Joni Mitchell is warbling from the stereo speakers. The rugby boys have come, out of curiosity and because like everyone else they have never been invited to a teacher's house before, even though it is a Saturday night and they could be at the club rooms. Jeff McDowell dispenses beer and vodka screwdrivers from the boot of his Ford Cortina. The whole class is at the barbecue, which is testament to Carly's popularity, and when one of the Christians tells Carly about Jeff McDowell's boot bar while she is in the front garden cooking sausages, she just smiles and says, 'If I see it, I'll confiscate it.'

Mark is drinking beer and Rima wonders if he is drinking so quickly so that he will get drunk enough to tell her how he feels. Natasha and Rima get a bit giggly on screwdrivers and start dancing to Carly's weird music. Carly brings the meat in from the garden and lays it out on the kitchen table with garlic bread and a gigantic coleslaw that has sunflower seeds in it. There is also a salad made with macaroni and peas and another made out of beans that Jeff McDowell says looks like it's been made out of Carly's necklaces. The rugby boys only eat the meat and garlic bread.

Natasha is drunk and Mark is also looking a little unsteady, but Carly doesn't seem to notice or care. After the food she gets up and dances and doesn't see when Jeff McDowell takes a fat joint out of his pocket. A group of them go down to the river and share it. Rima has never smoked pot before and can't believe how disgusting it tastes. Now Natasha is stoned and drunk and is dancing mock disco because someone has put on *Saturday Night Fever*. Rima wants to find Mark but he has disappeared. She wanders the room asking people if they have seen him and Jeff McDowell tries to pull her into a corner for a pash. The pot has made her feel like she is in a Pinter play where everything is slowed down and unreal. If she could find Mark she would feel better. She needs to talk to Carly too, because Natasha is supposed to be driving her home, but at the moment she is barely able to stand, let alone drive. Someone says they saw Mark go out the back door so Rima goes out to look for him. He could be outside choking on his own chunder for all Carly cares.

Rima stumbles out the back door and into the chill night. It is dark, very dark, with only a sliver of moon to guide her. She trips down the lawn towards the river and stops. She hears voices; a low murmur and a soft laugh, and can see a shape slumped up against a huge tree on the river's edge. The shape is moving strangely. Rima hurries forward and calls out. She calls again and is almost at the tree when the shape falls apart abruptly like something out of a horror film. She screams.

'What is it?' a woman's voice says sharply. 'What's wrong?' The voice belongs to Carly and the other part of the strange shape is Mark. The pot, the vodka and the two awkward bodies with their shadowy faces make Rima feel light-headed and giddy.

'Rima, what is wrong?' Carly asks again in a strangled voice and puts her hand on Rima's shoulders.

'Nothing,' Rima says, removing Carly's hand, 'I just came to tell you that I'm going home.'

Rima's mother is only in hospital for three weeks this time. She is assigned a new doctor, an Englishman who looks like a Heathcliff – Rima has just finished *Wuthering Heights* – with unruly hair and enigmatic eyes, who shakes all their hands when they arrive to take their mother home. He has asked that they all come in so he can discuss their mother's illness. Jenny comes too even though she is hardly a part of the family any more and is moving into a flat with Neil. She moans about how stuffy the room is. The doctor comes out from behind his desk and sits with them in their half-circle of chairs.

'I'm fairly certain,' he says, 'that Angela has been misdiagnosed and wrongly medicated all these years. We are trying a new drug that I think will make her well again.' The doctor's eyes are so forceful that Rima can't look at him and has to suppress the urge to giggle. She feels like she is in church or the headmaster's office.

'I believe that Angela suffers from manic depression, which can be successfully treated with a drug called Lithium, and we have noticed an improvement in her already.' Rima's father lets out a long breath and her mother shakes her head slowly.

'Are you saying that for ten years I've been taking the wrong drugs? Are you saying that?'

'Yes,' he says, and she starts to cry. Not the let-me-out-of-this-hell, desperate moaning she used to do for hours on end in her room, but a silent, sad, dabbing-the-corners-of-her-eyes and almost normal cry.

'How could that happen?' she says, shaking her head harder. 'How could Dr Weinburg get it so wrong?'

'Things are changing in mental health all the time,' the doctor says, looking uncomfortable for the first time. 'There is so much we still don't know, and Harold did what he thought was right.'

Rima's mother goes off to the ward to get her bags and the Heathcliff doctor walks them out. He shakes all their hands again and says something quietly to her father. Rima asks him what he said as they wait for their mother in the car park. Her father's hands are clenched into fists.

'He told me not to let her anywhere near Weinburg. He said he's about to be struck off the register for incompetence. But you know what, girls?'

The girls shake their heads but they both know.

'I might just kill him first.'

Natasha beats Rima by three marks in the Bursary English exam, but Rima doesn't care. Beating Natasha was mostly for Mark anyway and Mark is going back to live in Auckland. Carly is leaving too. She is going to teach at an alternative school in Wellington, where there is no uniform and the staff and attitudes are more progressive. Wendy and Shane are back together again, which Wendy says is pretty good except that he still tries to get her to smoke pot. Rima doesn't tell anyone – not even Wendy – about what she saw the night of the class barbecue. It seems like a long time ago and is all a bit of a blur and she has other more important things to think about now.

A man from Canterbury University comes to talk to them about courses and she pre-enrols in English Literature and Psychology. When she tells her family at the dinner table that night her father rolls his eyes and says, 'Psychology – you must be nuts,' and Bea, who's home for the summer break and already driving everyone crazy, tells Rima she's being selfish.

'You should be studying Sociology, not Psychology,' she says. 'Psychology is a cop-out. If you really want to change people's lives you have to work from the outside in.' While Bea is lecturing Rima, her father winks at her and steals the last piece of chicken off Bea's plate.

Rima still hasn't had sex and that's OK most of the time. Her mother tells her not to worry.

'If you haven't had it, it's because you're not ready or because you haven't met the right person, but he's out there, don't you worry. I can see him now, sitting in your Psychology lecture theatre waiting for you. He'll have tangled black hair with a strong jaw and brooding eyes; a cross between Mr Darcy and Heathcliff.'

'Shut up, Mum,' Rima says, and thinks about how good it will be when she leaves home.

# ELIZABETH SMITHER

Mark Dwyer/Daily News

Elizabeth Smither was the first woman Te Mata Estate Poet Laureate (2001–2003) but she has also written four collections of short stories and four novels, most recently *Different Kinds of Pleasure* (Penguin, 2005). A new collection of poems, *The Year of Adverbs,* was published by Auckland University Press in August.

# KATHY
# AND TIM

They met at Virginia Lake. Kathy was carrying a groovy purple snakeskin handbag, swinging it, though she had held it decorously at first as she approached the lake. But as she came nearer and the water gleamed and blurry shapes – there was something wrong with her eyes – resolved themselves into ducks, she swung it for comfort, as if she was trying to suggest ease.

It had been Tim's last try on DateMe, the last time ever that he would go searching on that meat market. He scrolled down face after face: bouffant hair, protuberant eyes, pleading disguised as defiance. What was wrong with these women, he asked himself. What was wrong with him? And yet, so often encounters in the flesh failed too. There had been a Table for Eight after which he had teamed up with the likeliest of an unlikely group. That had lasted through two coffees, a lunch with long pauses and the woman looking bored; finally dinner and a one-night stand from which both had been pleased to flee. But scrolling down, half-attentive, like examining a familiar menu when one is not hungry, there had been Kathy.

He stopped the scrolling motion at once, he reversed with a squeal of brakes. Surely there was nothing of artifice in those beautiful, slightly abashed eyes. I shouldn't, truly, be doing this, they seemed to say. She might have been in a police cell. What will my mother think? And yet somehow she had forced herself to face the camera. And her little bio – that had world-weariness in it as well, just the way he felt. *One last shot* was the subtext. *One more time and then I'll call it a day*.

And now her feet were crunching on the gravel path and her purple handbag was swinging from her wrist and it was too late to change motion. As if she had started a pendulum. He would be watching, she thought. Tim would be watching.

Tim too had started early. The city in which he lived was on the opposite side of the North Island, almost parallel to Kathy's city, but unable to be reached directly, so they swooped towards one another like birds. He had risen at 6 a.m., unable to sleep, showered and eaten a piece of half-blackened toast with raspberry jam. The roof of his mouth was slightly scalded by coffee.

By 7 a.m. he was in his car, driving south. He had hours in hand because the meeting was not until noon. High noon, he thought as he drove, more slowly than usual as if it were not only anticipation but he was farewelling stretches of landscape, each little town he passed through. He knew, whatever happened, he would come back changed. The thought of his old, his present, life made his stomach clench. No more trawling on the internet – that at least was gone. He would slink back and hope that one day one of his friends would introduce him to someone. But then, he reflected, that had already been tried and probably exhausted. No hostess would try more than twice, since it seemed a personal insult.

When he was fifty kilometres away from the lake – he wondered if *lake* held a significance, some Freudian meaning? – Tim stopped at a picnic area and sat overlooking a valley. Its gentle undulations led to a soft sky and a glimpse of the sea between hills. He sat for a long time, resting his eyes on the soft shapes. He ate a Mars bar and put the wrapper in the bin provided.

Kathy can see the lake clearly as she walks towards it. She half wishes she didn't. It's as if the lake, surrounded by reeds that look groomed, comes into view and expands in a way there is no turning back from. It resembles an eye that is glancing elsewhere, and now opens and focuses. Her purple handbag seems silly, an affectation. Tim, who is undoubtedly watching, will notice. He will consider it evidence of lack of character; he may not even stop long enough for her to explain that she bought it in a sale, that she was in a strange mood, half self-pity and half pity moving outwards, as the glint on the water moves, pity without an object. It's the same when she watches a sentimental movie. She fumbles for her handbag and presses a handkerchief to her eyes, she hopes her mascara hasn't run.

In the hot car, Kathy was sure her make-up had melted. She had debated stopping at a petrol station rest room and redoing her face. Instead she had simply refilled the tank and driven on. She has checked her lipstick in a little pink hand mirror and dabbed her cheeks with pressed powder.

A young man is approaching her from the other side of the lake. At first Kathy's eyes are too misted over to see properly. She can hear the crunch of his feet on the gravel; she will veer aside to let him pass. Then she sees that it must be Tim. The face is the face that she had brought up on her screen and then clicked to enlarge. He is a little shorter than she expected and his hair is in a different style: cut short and standing up like blades of grass. He must have given his height in centimetres and she had not registered. But the face, now looking at hers, smiling tentatively, as if his lips are dry, is the right face.

'I saw the handbag flashing through the trees,' he says when they are standing face-to-face, fifty centimetres or so apart, and the sounds of their gravel passages have died away, except for a few small stones that go on shifting.

'So you *were* watching,' Kathy says.

'I was a boy scout,' Tim replies.

'Your hair is different,' Kathy says.

'I thought it might give me height.'

'Better than cowboy boots,' Kathy says.

Somehow it doesn't seem to be going right. And yet, as they walk side by side along the path and then on to the grass, she is beginning to relax. There are ducks near the reeds, bobbing and making the dappled light move in time with their motion. The reeds gleam where the light touches them, and the little pavilion at the end of its boardwalk is stippled with sunlight and shadow.

'What time did you leave this morning?' Tim asks.

'Seven. I couldn't sleep,' Kathy replies.

'Seven. I couldn't sleep either.'

Hours to allow for punctures, change of heart, breakfast somewhere if anything could be faced. Stops looking at the landscape for answers. But the landscape never answered.

'Do you like ducks?' Kathy asks. Several had clambered up the bank and were shaking their wings. Others sit like decoy ducks on the grass.

'Yes,' Tim replies, though he doesn't know for sure. Is the conversation going to be reduced to this? Do you like Kathy? Do you like Tim?

They walk on a little further and find a wooden seat. Now the whole lake is spread in front of them, so they sense not just its glittering, moving, wind-touched surface, but the way it sits in the earth like a bowl surrounded by waving grasses and reeds. A couple is walking along the wooden slats to the little pavilion. A toddler with a piece of bread in his hand stumbles towards a group of ducks. Kathy shakes her head slightly to rid herself of notions of marriage and children. And on cue a slight shade falls; the couple turn and the toddler trips and drops the bread. At that moment Tim reaches out his hand and covers Kathy's with his. It feels warm, like a tortoise under its shell. 'Relax,' he says. 'We have the whole day.'

Above the lake is a café in a large, old-fashioned house, a villa with bay windows and white verandahs. To reach it they have to cross a busy road and Tim takes Kathy's elbow. And if there were no road, she thinks, there would be no elbow. How often does she think like this, of serendipity. If there had been no lake, no conveniently placed park bench, no ducks to distract so she peered at them like a naturalist. And now, seated at a window table, they can look out over the lake from a bird's perspective. The ducks describe a pattern, like a flotilla, and seem purposeful.

Kathy reaches out her hand and touches her purple snakeskin handbag which is lying at her feet. She looks enviously at Tim's smooth, clean-shaven cheeks. He has nice skin, she tells herself. Not dry but not oily either. She prays, when eventually she will have to excuse herself 'to powder her nose' – that ridiculous expression, as if the world is full of female noses searching for powder – that she has brought everything. The little cylinder of concealer with its applicator under the lid, the cotton bud for Infallible – Resists Signs of Fatigue – make-up which she might need to hastily smear on her cheeks and forehead, the new lipstick in the shade called Crushed Velvet.

She raises her eyes and Tim is looking at her. His eyes are brown, duck coloured, velvety. They are rounder in shape than hers. Hers are wider and narrower, golden-brown.

'It's all a bit of a shock,' he says, as he lifts the lid of the teapot and peers inside to see how many teabags there are. There are two, which seems a good sign.

'I think I'm getting a bit of a reaction,' Kathy admits. 'All the build-up, the anticipation. Why I was on the net in the first place.'

'The early start,' Tim adds. 'I don't think I've ever driven so slowly or so badly. My hands felt clammy.'

'And if you hadn't been surfing last Wednesday. When you said you were a librarian as well . . .'

'I didn't log on until Thursday morning. I couldn't sleep. I'd been at a nightclub and it was my day off. I thought if I don't press the flesh, get in touch with real people, however disagreeable. I had a thumping headache. And then you popped up on the screen. I thought you looked startled at being there. You couldn't sell yourself, that was obvious.'

Kathy is never going to tell Tim that she has had over thirty replies, that uncertainty is not a deterrent. Then she wonders how many replies he had, how many faces and figures were discarded. What drew you to me, she wants to ask, but it is too early. And *is* he drawn? For she can tell he is courteous, polite, and that if he does not see her after today, his withdrawal will be polite as well.

Kathy has chosen an asparagus roll and a miniature muffin: nothing dangerous. She had thought of a neenish tart but then wondered if the filling might run. Tim is eating a sausage roll and a little cake shaped like a boat with icing and a cherry. What shall we do now, Kathy wonders, and her heart beats in her chest like a bird.

'What would you like to do next?' Tim asks. 'It's funny, I had it thought out. The lake, a walk, but now I realise I haven't. Would you like to go for a drive? Your car or mine?'

So they go to inspect each other's cars. Tim's low-slung red Mazda MX5, Kathy's rust-spotted white Nissan Primera. But first, since they are parked on opposite sides of the lake, Kathy goes to fetch hers and bring it nearer to Tim's. She walks away from him, swinging her handbag, fumbling in it for the keys.

Tim drives his sports car away from the lake and out into the country. The MX5 eats up the miles and Kathy's hair blows in the breeze. The purple handbag sits at her feet. She looks at Tim's hands, their shape: square fingertips, supposed to represent someone good with money, straight fingers through which thought, and perhaps impulse, flows. How impulsive is he, she wonders, and then she considers her own behaviour, looks down at her starfish-shaped hands, the nails buffed and shiny and painted with a pink nail polish that glitters. She thinks of putting a hand over Tim's hand on the wheel, then she desists.

Soon they are at the picnic space at which Tim stopped on the way to the lake. The same hills like a stage set, slightly deeper gradations of colour.

A mynah bird is pecking in a wire rubbish bin. There are two apples on the back seat and Tim reaches over, rubs one on his sleeve and hands it to Kathy. Now they are sitting opposite each other at a wooden table with fixed seats, biting into the flesh of two Splendour apples.

'Adam and Eve,' Kathy says.

'Kathy and Tim.'

'It all seems so sudden.'

'The apples?' Tim asks.

'No.' (Taking a risk.) 'The liking.'

'Buffoon.'

And Kathy, who is a faster eater, throws her apple core past Tim's ear. Then they are standing under a tree – not an apple, a beech tree – and finding how well their bodies match. Not quite shoulder to shoulder – Tim is taller – but at thigh and hip, flesh and bone. As if their bodies have been designed for each other. Kathy's flesh feels soft and warm, Tim's feels dense and warm. Something billows about them in clouds, breezes, the earth spins a little and then settles.

After the kiss Kathy looks up and checks the landscape again. Hill behind hill, meadow leading to hill, dandelions dancing in the foreground, as if the tremor has passed through them too.

'What shall we do now?' Tim asks. He'd like to go to a motel. It feels so certain. They could sign false names in the register. Kathy could avert her eyes and fumble in her handbag while Tim says, Tim Webb and Kathy Honeyfield. With some indecipherable signature. No, it would have to be a made-up name in case someone, but he can't think who it might be, looks at the register later. A detective sent by Kathy's parents, a Pinkerton detective sent by his mother who is a great thriller reader. Longingly he thinks of the hotels in France where liaisons are catered for: two lovers embracing on the Boulevard Saint-Michel and then slipping through a doorway, climbing the stairs hand-in-hand, with the man holding a heavy key. On his only visit to Paris Tim had noticed the weightiness of the keys, the insistence that they not leave the hotel.

Or there is the lake with its shining surface. Perhaps they could lie down, like ducks, amid the reeds. They could look like a couple having a picnic, surreptitiously removing items of clothing, kicking off their shoes, undoing a blouse button. If anyone came past Kathy could pretend to swat him with her handbag, like an Edwardian farce.

But if that was what he wanted, Tim reflects, they could stay here. They could climb over the stile and walk in the meadow and find a spot. Kathy could carry her shoes.

'I wish . . .' Tim begins, 'but it is too soon.'

'What is it you wish?' Kathy asks.

'It is too soon for my wish.'

'Who says it is too soon?' she replies.


There is a little motel in a side street whose entrance is partially obscured by nikau palms. The sign, El Dorado Motor Inn, has seen better days, and Tim suspects that if it were night some of the neon letters might not light up. Tim carries his attaché case which he has taken from the back seat and Kathy has her handbag. It hardly constitutes luggage. Perhaps they will pass for a business couple, meeting out of town. But the woman at the desk seems singularly disinterested. Tim manages to stop himself muttering something about getting the luggage from the car later.

'One night?' she asks. 'That's the minimum.' Perhaps she does have an inkling.

Neither had thought of staying the night. The plan was to meet at the lake, spend a few hours together and drive back to their respective cities. If they liked each other they would phone and arrange another meeting.

This new complication means two phone calls claiming sick leave.

Compassionate leave, Kathy thinks, when they are finally in one of the rooms in an annexe out the back. There is a courtyard and more palm trees. The walls are concrete block, painted a searing white. The bedcover is brown, the carpet flecked. The curtains seem as if they might not quite close in the middle.

'I haven't a toothbrush,' Kathy says, looking at her face in the bathroom mirror – flushed, wide-eyed like some animal.

'We'll go to the chemist,' Tim says. 'And we can go out for dinner or order a pizza.'

'Go out,' Kathy says. Now she is in it, the motel seems rather oppressive.

Tim goes in search of a chemist: he will buy two toothbrushes and two sachets of shampoo as well as the obvious – chemists, he decides, must make a lot of money on purchases that surround packets of condoms. He had brought nothing, not daring to hope, feeling that there was a kind of purity involved – how often had he carried one in his wallet only to have it looking up at him like an uncashed banknote. There is a display of perfumed soap just before he reaches the counter – another strategy, no doubt – and he buys a cake of lavender and manuka honey soap. He passes a dairy on the way back, goes in and buys a single sunflower in a purple wrapper. He has seen the look on Kathy's face when she stood at the bedroom door.

Romance has to be *made*, Tim thinks as, arms full, he heads back. The door of unit seven is open slightly and Kathy is sitting on a formica chair, holding a black cat in her arms.

They don't go out in the end. A pizza delivery boy unpacks a small Gourmet Tropical and a Seafood Supreme from his saddlebag, accepts Tim's tip, and drives away in a scatter of pebbles. Kathy peels off a piece of bacon and feeds it to the black cat. Tim puts the shrimps he has failed to tell Kathy about on the side of his plate. Kathy takes tiny little bites, nibbles really, of her pizza, eating the point of the triangle first. There are some little bottles of wine in the refrigerator as well as orange juice and milk.

'I should have brought some champagne,' Tim says. 'I was too preoccupied.'

'I like it that you don't plan,' Kathy confides. 'When I was young I used to think it was a sign of sincerity.' She has been burnt since.

'I planned a better place. Perhaps this was a silly idea.'

'No,' says Kathy. And now she tips the cat off her lap and resolutely closes the lid of the pizza box. She takes Tim's plate with its decoration of pink shrimps and heads into the kitchen. He hears a tap running, the lid of the kitchen tidy close. It could be the beginning of a Beethoven symphony.

Then Kathy is back. She lays a hand on his shoulder – how soft it is he can tell through the material of his shirt.

'Come,' she says.

How well Kathy and Tim fit together. First they fold their clothes on a chair – neither wants the uncouthness of tearing them off. What if Tim loses a button and Kathy has to rummage through the drawers to find a sewing kit (unlikely). And in any case it is too early and this slowness of undressing imparts a kind of ceremony. But then they turn to each other and the fit begins: head to toe, hand to hair, as if each is giving a laying on of hands, the scent and feel of each other's skins – Tim's is slightly, pleasantly oily, just the faintest oiliness like baby oil added to a bath – Kathy doesn't think she could bear dry skin. When the warmth comes to both their skins, that seems matched too, an equal heat rising from the first look they exchanged, when Kathy was walking towards Tim, swinging her purple handbag.

The photo Kathy had posted on DateMe had been taken by her mother, Dianne. This was the reason it was so relaxed, so open-looking. Everything about it was open: the expression in the eyes, partly deprecating, amused, as if Kathy and her mother were conspirators. Her freshly washed, beautiful hair – the next thing Tim would notice after the handbag, his eyes would linger on its rich, golden-brown, foxy colour – fell over the shoulders of her blouse and a few light strands waved across her face. Kathy felt she could not do it without her mother's knowledge. Someone to go through the hits and vet them, someone with more experience to read between the lines.

Tim, after what he felt was one of the dreariest days of

his life, had switched on DateMe when he got back to his darkened house. He went to the screen with his hopes as horizontal as a deceased's heart monitor. And then Kathy had sprung out: her open face, her open text. *I wish to meet*, she had written.

Not *I want* as so many began, like Wanted posters for felons. Tim read *I wish to meet* as a prayer that, if it were not answered, would remain in place, patiently seeking. There were just a few sentences. He memorised them after he had composed his own spontaneous answer – it felt white-hot, a surprise to him, who always considered everything he wrote. *I feel drawn to you*, he typed. *I can't tell why. I don't want to promise too much. I should very much like a chance to meet.*

Even entangled in bedsheets – poor quality Dacron, bad colour choice: navy-blue to which lint clings like very distant stars in a dark-blue heaven – Kathy and Tim feel comfortable. A few pizza crumbs, a flake of dried bacon, is added to the sheets, for Tim has gone to the fridge and brought the last two slices on a plate.

Somehow the shabbiness of the room makes their love blaze. For that is what it feels like as the sun begins to lighten and warm the room and all the things that lie ahead: the drive home, the phone calls that both are sure – almost sure – will certainly follow. Already Kathy sees herself at her mother's house, standing in the hallway, her hand resting on the back of a chair, as she talks. Her mother will go past and pull a face and Kathy will pull one in return, so her voice sounds distorted for a moment and Tim will ask if she is all right.

Eventually Tim brings a second cup of tea and pulls the spare pillows from the top of the wardrobe. They lie back against them. Kathy feels like crooking her little finger as she lifts the plain white cup to her lips. Then Tim takes it from her and they slide down into the dark-blue sheets again, among the pizza crumbs, the little crumb of bacon, a few flakes of salt, the scent of their bodies.

It is harder leaving the motel than arriving since neither feels so assured. Kathy walks straight to Tim's car and Tim hands back the key. In the car Kathy clutches her handbag, rearranges some of the contents. She puts on fresh lipstick and checks her hair. She lets out a big sigh, of happiness or fatigue, she cannot tell. She looks at Tim walking towards her – fatigued and joyful as she is, she thinks – and she measures him against his photograph on DateMe. His hair is standing up a little and there is a fine patina of perspiration on his brow. Ladies glow, she thinks. But the real glow is in the heart. She looks at his hands on the steering wheel, the fine oval fingernails that are cut short and square, in the recommended manner of those licensed to touch: surgeons and gynaecologists.

'You're blushing,' Tim says, looking at her.

Tim drives Kathy to the parking lot at Virginia Lake to collect her car. She opens the driver's door and puts her handbag on the seat. Then she closes the door and stands facing Tim. They wrap their arms around each other, Kathy's arms around Tim's waist, Tim's arms higher up, touching her shoulder blades. Kathy doesn't move, even if the next move is a kiss. The world is full of people wanting time to move and some few wanting it to stand still.

Then she wrenches herself out of his arms, avoiding the kiss, leaving Tim bewildered, fumbles with the car and starts the motor.

'I'll phone you tonight,' she calls and then, since he still looks bewildered, she takes one hand off the wheel and blows him a kiss.

She doesn't register the streets that lead swiftly to the highway, nor does she register the highway itself, though she regards the centre marking, the countryside as it begins, the trees she gazed on twenty-four hours earlier with such attention. She passes the picnic stops, the long views, the fields with animals grazing. She slows automatically at pedestrian crossings and little towns. But she thinks of nothing, all thought is held back, a storehouse to be opened later.

Dianne Honeyfield comes in from the garden with the last cherry tomatoes in her hands as Kathy's car pulls up. She resists the impulse to go and meet her; she arranges her face into a neutral expression, ready to go either way. She hears her daughter's footsteps, something – perhaps a handbag – being set down. Then Kathy's arms are circling her waist and tears are running down her face.

'Was it all right?' Dianne asks.

*'Oh, was it all right!'* Kathy replies.

Tim likewise drives home in a daze. He drives through flatter country, sheep instead of cows. Fruit trees proliferate as he comes nearer the coast. Finally there is his seaside city with its line of guardian pines, the perpetual mist rising from the breaking waves. In a storm this mist seems to fling people against their houses, they walk as if in a blizzard. Tim has no one to meet him and he is grateful. He too had refused to think of Kathy as he drove. He takes a shower and stands dreamily under it until the hot water runs out and a sudden dash of cold causes him to leap out.

★

They talk. They talk about everything. Three hours the first night. Two hours, forty-three minutes the second. Dianne Honeyfield stands in the doorway, pointing to her watch. Kathy rolls her eyes in return. She pushes a curl back from her forehead, she twines a long golden strand around her fingers.

'I'll call you tomorrow,' Tim says.

Already, in his lunch hour, he has stopped at a jewellers and looked at engagement rings. He wishes he had measured Kathy's finger. He thinks she might prefer a solitaire, then changes his mind to a band of small diamonds. They need to watch stars together, to ascertain if she prefers single stars to constellations.

At work in the Genealogy and Reference Room, Tim can hardly concentrate. Luckily he has several long searches to occupy him and the usual quota of aggrieved family history seekers. What if they do discover a bishop, an explorer, a minor poet? Sometimes Tim longs to tell them to get on with their own lives, that the illustrious ancestors whose luminosity they seek did not bend over microfilm readers, dreaming their lives away.

But today he is almost grateful for the tedium, above which his thoughts rise and float, a list of possibilities, all rich in potential. One of his regulars has discovered she is related to a highwayman and lets out a shriek.

'I can't think of anything more desirable,' Tim says when he finds her transfixed. 'A big black horse, a cloak, matching pistols.'

'But he might have been hanged,' the woman says, and Tim surmises her family researches might be at an end.

He carries the image of the highwayman throughout the day.

'I found someone a highwayman,' he says to Kathy that night.

'That reminds me a bit of you,' she replies.

'Only a bit?' he asks, and in his own hallway he lifts one leg onto a little ornate chair and stands in a highwayman pose.

'You didn't go to bed too soon?' Dianne Honeyfield asks. She has a liberal heart underpinned by half-ignored strictures. To go to bed is natural, whatever comes after. But she likes to think of her daughter being rewarded and surely there are rewards in waiting.

'I thought as you do. I didn't intend to,' Kathy says, when they are drinking hot chocolate at the kitchen table.

'And now you are rewarded,' her mother says. 'Since he phones every night.'

'I'll pay my share of the phone,' Kathy says. 'Even if it takes half my salary.'

'No,' Dianne says, and the protest arises from somewhere deep inside. 'I'm going to insist on that. Whatever happens in the future let me have this much share of it. I'm going to pay the phone bill.'

'You'll like my mother,' Kathy says the next night when Tim phones. Two hours, twelve minutes. They are both going to have an early night. While they sleep the well of their conversation fills up again. Tim is nearly asleep, his hand has turned off the bed lamp when he thinks this. And then, like a seer, he foretells the future. A table decorated with roses and ferns. A silver bucket with beaded drops and the protruding neck of a champagne bottle.

# CHARLOTTE GRIMSHAW

Charlotte Grimshaw is the author of three critically acclaimed novels, *Provocation* and *Guilt*, published in Britain and New Zealand, and *Foreign City*, and a short story collection, *Opportunity*. In 2000 she was awarded the Buddle Findlay Sargeson Fellowship. She was a double finalist, and prizewinner, in the 2005 *Sunday Star-Times* Short Story Competition, and in 2006 she won the Bank of New Zealand Katherine Mansfield Premier Writer's Award for short fiction. Her short stories have appeared in, among others, *The Best New Zealand Fiction* Volumes 2 and 3, the *New Zealand Listener*, the *Sunday Star-Times*, Reed Publishing's *Myth of the 21st Century*, and *Stand* magazine in Britain. She lives in Auckland.

# THE YARD BROOM

It had started to get hot as soon as the sun rose. I got up early and went out onto the deck. A few stars hung on the horizon, but the sky was turning to pale blue and the air was thick with a haze of dust and seeds. The plants and trees were motionless. There had been no wind for a week, just the heat and the cloudless sky, the land burnt brown by the drought. The skin of the bay was smooth and glassy. In the distance the dunes of the white beach seemed to hang in the air above the dried-out swamp and the hill, recently burnt by a scrub fire, stood out black against the banks of pure white sand. A truck rumbled along the road, raising dust. A dog wandered under the gum trees. I went to the bathroom and looked at my face in the mirror. There was the sunburnt skin, the straw hair, blue eyes, and the black shadow that had risen in the night under my right eye, dark and ugly as the burnt hill in the distance. I touched it, and felt it throb. A phrase came into my mind. 'The last straw . . .'

Nathan was lying on his side, asleep, his muscular arm with its tattooed circle of barbed wire resting along his body. He had a small, neat face, even-featured, with a tidy, curving mouth. His head was shaved; he wore a bone carving round his neck. His hand, the fingers loosely curled, was black with tattoos, and there was a small star tattooed on his cheek below his eye. His fingernails were broken and black from work, as were mine. We couldn't get the grease and grime out of them, and after a while we gave up trying.

Last night we'd gone to a party deep in the pine forest. I hadn't wanted to go; the people who lived in the forest were like bandits, they lived in tumbledown shacks surrounded by dead cars; they made their money by growing dope and trading drugs. They were Nathan's cousins but I was afraid of them. I'd tried to make excuses but he'd persuaded me to go, and I'd driven there with him in the ute and sat out on the deck with toothless Mereana, who rolled joints on her knee while slapping away the howling kids who tottered around her, crying for attention. 'Get off, I'll give you a hiding,' she threatened, whacking their heads, grinning, smacking her lips. She looked demented, though there was an intelligent, malignant gleam in her eye. I offered to put two of the smaller children to bed. She shrugged and went on rolling her joints. When I took the stinking toddlers inside I couldn't find where they were supposed to sleep. I put them in a double bed. Outside, people were already drunk and stoned.

I lifted up the blind. The house lights shone across the clearing, making shadows of the hulks of dead cars, and beyond that the trees rose like a black wall. The trees crowded around the house, suffocating it, shutting out the light. Anything could happen out here.

Nathan had been shifty all evening – he was up to something with Mereana's husband, Huru Wright. I couldn't stand Huru. When he looked at you, it was like being watched by an animal. His expression was intent and cold, also blunted and damaged, as if all feeling had been beaten out of him. He was long-haired and short and squat; his shoulders sloped like an ape's. When he smiled, it gave you a shock. He looked as though he were thinking over some horrible, pleasurable, secret idea.

I glanced down at the two kids. They were silent, staring, not moving. I thought, they'll be just like their parents. Little killers. As I got up, one of them started to cry. He had no choice being here, but why did I go on living in the settlement? I heard Nathan calling me. I pulled the boy's small hand off my arm and went out. I sat on the deck and drank beer.

There was a fight – two men squaring off, their shadows playing on the ground, until one struggled free from the other and ran straight into the blackness of the trees. His opponent stumbled back to the deck and went on drinking. The other man stayed out there, watching perhaps, just outside the circle of light. That was what bothered me about the place, people huddling in the light and the blackness all around, so that everything was compressed into a hellish little space, and always the feeling that something cold and immovable was watching. I put my hand on Nathan's and said, 'Let's go, before . . .'

It was hours before we went, and when we did he was so drunk and stoned he could barely keep on the road. Dust and pine needles and insects whirled in the headlights. He hit a bluff and we stalled and I sat while he cursed and struggled to start the engine. I saw shapes just outside the lights. He began to accuse me of crazy things, keeping secrets from him, spying.

'Huru says you sit there just looking at people,' he said. 'Staring at them, like you're taking notes.'

Something he'd talked about with Huru had made him paranoid. 'It's freaky out here,' he said, setting off too fast, so that we crashed and bumped on the rough surface, risking another stall or a crash into the clay bank.

We drove out of the forest. Now we could see the sky and the blazing stars, and the dry, barren scrubland in the moonlight. The moon was shining on the sea down at the bay, and there was a boat going out, sending a beam of light across the water. The camping ground was full of caravans and tents, and there were torches on the beach – people fishing or going for a late-night swim.

'You don't like Huru, do you?' Nathan said unpleasantly.

'You know I don't. What's to like? His good looks?'

He said quietly, 'He's my cousin.'

'I don't have to like him. Anyway, you don't like him either.'

'So I can't trust you then.' His voice took on a self-righteous whine. He drummed his fingers on the wheel. His expression, when he glanced at me, was very bad.

'Come on,' I pleaded. 'You're being paranoid. You can trust me.'

'I might have things I need to keep to myself . . .' He gulped and cleared his throat, as if his mouth had gone dry. The ute swerved.

'Hey, you idiot. Watch it!'

'*You* watch it,' he shouted. He slammed on the brakes and slapped me on the side of the head. Stars exploded in my eyes.

He looked stunned. 'Sorry,' he whispered, and reached out his hand. I pushed him away. We sat in silence. There was a fire down on the beach and we could hear people singing.

It was early morning, but I could tell it was going to be hot. Wavy lines of heat rippled up from the dry, brown land. There were little tornadoes of dust in the distance as cars drove along the main road. I put on my shorts and boots and reflector jacket and walked down to the dump. This was the only place for rubbish disposal in the settlement. There was no collection; people had to bring the rubbish in themselves. There was already a pile of bags at the gates, left by people who couldn't be bothered waiting for us to open. I collected as many as I could, dragging them along to our office, a shipping container, where we sheltered from the rain and the heat, and kept our gear. The dump had been overhauled – people used to throw everything into a single large container, which was then taken away by truck. Now we were called a Recycling Station, and the rubbish was sorted into types, and people had to pay to deposit their loads. Nathan and I worked fulltime sorting the rubbish and taking fees. In the summer the baches and camping grounds were full and there was a huge amount to be sorted; in the winter we dealt with the rubbish from the permanent residents.

Nathan turned up in the ute. I started on the bottles. I could tell when a car was approaching by the clouds of dust, and when it drove onto the site I came out of the shade of the office and took the bags and the fee. The locals arrived in their beaten-up cars and were lazy and messy, and tried to avoid paying. The holiday people had good cars and were conscientious about what they handed over. These shiny city people – even their rubbish was tidy. It was always the same: the kids, grumpy and hot from being in the car, would open the door and I'd hear the chorus of reedy little voices, 'Pooh! It stinks. Oh phwoar!' and then the giggling and the squabbling between those who wanted the window open, and those who couldn't stand the pong. It was bad all right. Not only did the bins give off a terrible reek but the land itself, especially in summer, was soaked with layers of rubbish, so that the stink came up in waves from the ground and hung on the hot air. The few trees were decorated with paper that had blown out of the bins, and the land around was so barren and dry that it increased the sense of dreariness and squalor. The men avoided my eye, paid their fee and jumped back in the car. The women sat behind the glass and stared.

I used to hate the smell. Now I didn't notice. The fact that I'd stopped noticing it bothered me for a while; I thought I might smell bad after work and not realise. But Nathan and I led the same life here as everyone else, going to parties and hangis and tangis and to the pub in town, and no one had ever given me any trouble (or told me I stank). But the stares of the holiday women – I minded them. They took no notice of Nathan. A Maori rubbishman. Poor Nathan, they assumed he was where he belonged.

What they saw: I was nineteen, with blonde hair and blue eyes. I wore a filthy sleeveless reflector jacket over shorts and a T-shirt, and heavy boots with short, thick socks. I had crude blue tattoos on my forearms, a bracelet tattooed on my wrist. My hands were dry and filthy, my fingernails broken. I wore no make-up. My skin was streaked with dust. My eyes were bloodshot and one of them was blackened and swollen nearly shut. My co-worker and, since he was the one I was seen with in the settlement, the probable deliverer of the black eye, worked nearby looking hung-over and shame-faced, casting miserable looks my way and hoiking into the bins. A fine pair we were.

The morning dragged on. The cars drove up in a whirl of dust, unloaded their bags and drove away. Nathan worked without talking. I could tell he felt bad about what he'd done, but there was something secretive in his expression that worried me.

A couple arrived in an SUV. She was holding a map. He got out and went round to get out the rubbish.

I took the bags. 'You off home?'

'Back to Auckland.'

'I used to live in Auckland.'

'Really?' He was backing away, with a prissy little smile. The woman stared.

'Yeah, bugger off then,' I said under my breath. They drove away.

'Go and get us some lunch,' I told Nathan. He slunk off. I'd always been able to tell him what to do. He might break out and lose his temper, but he loved me and was afraid I would leave. I had that power over him.

But lately, Nathan had been spending a lot of time in the forest with Huru. I'd asked him about it and he'd only worked himself into a state and told me to mind my own business. Huru had it in for me. He whispered in Nathan's ear, spooked him. Nathan was nervous and susceptible; he believed in ghosts and spirits and tapu. As far as I was concerned Huru was just a lowlife and a criminal, but he came on like a witch doctor, like a tohunga. And I had one specific worry: that

Huru would introduce Nathan to smoking P.

Nathan came back with the lunch. He thought for a moment. 'Huru says . . .'

I took the food and said coaxingly, 'Nathan, you shouldn't go out there. They're bad. Stick with your own.' I meant the other side of his family who lived around the bay. They were respectable, they took diligent care of their marae, they fund-raised for the Maori Party. They all had jobs.

He gave me a sour look. He said, 'You think I want to spend the rest of my life in a dump?'

My great-grandfather was Dutch. He was from Indonesia, where he'd been a rich landowner and a specialist in tropical horticulture. He was interned by the Japanese in the war, and then he came to New Zealand and settled in Auckland. My grandmother was born here and became a schoolteacher. My mother grew up in Auckland and went to university, but before she'd finished her degree she met my father, who was doing a degree in fine arts. He'd come out from Germany in his early twenties, and decided he wanted to stay here and be a painter. My mother got pregnant and dropped out of university. She worked in a bookshop. At some stage she and her friends started experimenting with drugs, and by the time I was about seven she was an addict.

We lived in a flat in Grafton. My father stayed home and painted, and she went to the bookshop. She was fired one Christmas for being stoned at work and falling off her chair. She got addicted to speed, and soon she was paranoid all the time. My father tried to help her. He also threatened to leave, taking me with him.

One weekend my father drove out to Piha with a friend, intending to take photographs for his work. They went for a swim at low tide. The surf was dangerously rough, and a wave picked him up and dumped him on his head on the sea bottom, injuring the vertebrae in his neck. He wasn't able to get out of the water, and he drowned.

My mother began to lose control. One day she arrived at school at lunchtime, very agitated, and insisted I must go home with her. A little scene developed. Summoning the teacher, she pointed at the sky and confided, in a hoarse whisper, 'See that helicopter? It's been following me *all day*.' That exchange set the teachers thinking, and I was taken away from her while she went into an expensive rehabilitation programme that my grandmother paid for. I lived with my grandmother until she came out.

Some time later she found herself a boyfriend. He got a job in a law firm in Australia, and we went too, supposedly to follow him. We never did catch up with him. We lived in Sydney until she answered an advertisement for a job in a hotel at Ayers Rock.

I remember flying in over the great rock, the land around it dry and red, like – I imagined – the surface of Mars. The sense of isolation, after flying over the immense desert, and the heat struck us as soon as we walked down the steps of the plane. At Ayers Rock there was a tiny settlement: four linked hotels, a camping ground, a small shopping centre and a few houses for the staff who worked in the hotels. I thought I would see some Aborigines but we soon discovered they were kept out of sight. There was a tourist show, where they had a didgeridoo and talked about the rock, Uluru, and its spiritual significance to the local people, but the brown guide and the brown man who played the didgeridoo were Maoris from Otara. Pamphlets in the hotels told guests they were paying a tax to protect the 'fragile community' of indigenous people, as if they were creatures, exotic animals. The workers regarded the Aborigines with contempt. They wouldn't work, they said. They were too drunk. When they did appear they usually *were* drunk, poor things. But you hardly saw them. My mother said New Zealand was a much healthier scene, as far as race relations went.

She tried to keep away from temptation. She worked on the reception desk at one of the hotels. She had a fling with the guide from Otara, but he was working his way through all the women in the place, and she got sick of that. Then she met Travis, who drove the bus that took tourists to and from the airport and out into the National Park.

We had a small house in the residential area. It looked like a bunker, with a low, curving roof, round windows and a concrete back porch. I could never get used to the stillness and quiet. In those few little roads nothing moved, no cars went past, there was no wind, and all around us the vast desert stretched away into the silence. At sunset Uluru was lit up with blazing red light, its sides striped with soft, rippling black shadows, and when night came the sky was filled with big, bright stars. I was supposed to be doing correspondence school but I spent a lot of time outside, exploring the red paths that ran across the hot, dry landscape. I was in a daze most of the time. Out in the National Park there were lizards, dingoes, spiders, snakes. The heat was ferocious. I missed my school at home, my friends. I was lonely. I had a sense of unreality. I used to stand outside the bunker in the vast, black, silent night, dreaming about home. I would have done anything to get away from my mother, and Travis.

She stayed clean, but it was hard. She was a gentle, nervous person. Travis started to be irritable and to push her around. When they'd finished their shifts he swaggered over to our house and behaved as if he owned it. He had a deep, harsh voice and a square jaw; he lifted weights and boasted about his strength; he was relentless, charmless. At least I thought so. I urged my mother to stand up to him, but she would pace and tremble and often she would turn on me. 'You're just like your father,' she'd say. 'You've got a will of iron.' She looked at me coldly, as if I was just another oppressor. Or she would throw things and scream, 'Why doesn't everybody leave me alone?'

After these scenes I would go outside and push a yard broom up and down the length of the porch, shifting the red dust, counting the steps to myself, ten steps forward, ten steps back. I remember it as a strange, compelling ritual: the broom, the red dust, ten steps forward, ten steps back. I would keep it up for a long time, until everything merged and nothing existed but red earth, silence, heat shimmer, shadows on the red rock.

My mother started taking sips of Travis's beers. He egged her on. She moved to drinking wine, and then spirits. It wasn't long before she was sacked and we flew back to Sydney. She worked in the Ascot Hotel in Kings Cross, and when she was fired from there she started working in a brothel. (She insisted she was a 'receptionist'.) After that fell through, we went back to Auckland.

I came home with the idea that something significant had happened to me at Uluru. On those silent afternoons, as I was pushing the yard broom up and down the concrete porch, I'd lost my grip. I finished school by some miracle and embarked on a vague attempt at university, but I had an affair with a married man that went horribly wrong, and one day after an argument I hitchhiked down the southern motorway and finished up in Wellington, which ended my university career.

Back in Auckland, I moved into a flat with a group of people who were busy, I soon discovered, setting the record for the most armed robberies performed in a year. The papers ran a series for a while, 'Today's armed robbery', which was a way of needling the police about their failure to make any arrests. My flatmate, an outwardly respectable blonde called Amanda, was the getaway driver. This I learned later, when the police kicked down the door. My flatmates were arrested, and the landlord threw me out. My mother had gone to try her luck in Australia again. My grandparents were dead. My father's family was in Europe. I had no one.

I moved in with Hemi, who lived in a tinny house. I didn't work. I applied for the dole. I cut tattoos in my arms. Hemi was feckless, sweet natured and extremely kind. He was the leader of a local street gang that had a ferocious reputation. It used to amuse me, travelling about with this terrible lot, who affected the mannerisms of American gangsters and frightened everyone they met. I was so starved of human warmth that I soaked up Hemi's kindness. But I was disgusted with myself. We were idle, directionless; we stayed up all night and slept all day. I never saw the sun.

Hemi and I and some of his gang drove up north for a tangi. In the car I listened, tranced with boredom, to their inane chatter. We stopped at a café in Kamo that backed onto a Christian camp. The camp advertised hot pools, and Hemi decided to try them. He and I went in, and he wanted to have sex beside the bubbling spa pool. It was a wet, squalid, ugly little room, with mouldy concrete pipes roaring in the walls. After a while I left him in there and came out into the car park. It was hot and bright, the cars flashing past on the open road. I had a crushing sense of inertia, disgust and squalor. I saw a man standing in the doorway of the Christian camp, carrying a backpack. I asked him, 'Where's the nearest bus station? I want to get away from here.'

His name was Pastor Kyle Sendells. I got into his car, without a word to anyone. Pastor Kyle drove me up to the Far North, where I met Nathan, and where I'd been ever since, at the dump. I never saw Hemi again.

My great-grandfather's house in Indonesia was large and grand. He was rich, well educated, by all accounts handsome and suave. His wife was 'delicate' and had only one child, my grandmother. She never recovered from the change of country, and died relatively young. I thought about how they'd made their way out here after their home was taken from them, how they'd tried to make a new life, and where the lines of their family had ended – in my case, in a sea of rubbish bags at the far end of the world.

And yet I believed I'd reached the lowest point of my life that day at the Christian camp at Kamo. The disgust, shame and weariness were overpowering. I had faith that I would never feel that low again, and that faith started when I was sitting in the car with Pastor Kyle Sendells, leaving Hemi mile after mile behind.

Pastor Kyle started his religious patter as soon as we were on the road. I was brought up an atheist and didn't pay any attention to it, but some of the things he said were useful, I have to admit. I was so low and depressed that I told him everything. It came out in a stream of despair. He was an intense, thin, wiry man, aged in his fifties, with deep lines down his face, blond hair and pale, sly eyes with fair eyelashes. He had on a faded checked shirt, nylon trousers and cheap shoes with zips. I told him about my mother, my father's death, about Travis who'd pushed my mother around and turned her back to booze and drugs, about trying and failing to live a decent life. I even told him about pushing the yard broom up and down the porch at Uluru, and how I believed that was the point when I'd lost my mind. He listened, and whenever I paused he chipped in. 'If we invite Jesus into our life,' he said, 'if we accept that he died for our sins . . .' He must have thought I was the ideal person for him to practise on – people do turn to God when they're low – but I was absolutely immune to the Lord.

When we stopped at a café, he sat down and stared at me, calculating, with his sly, pale eyes.

He said, 'Number one. You feel your mother's addiction has tainted you.'

'I don't,' I said.

He spread out his freckly hands and looked at them.

'Was your father an addict?'

'No.'

'Addiction can be inherited. But if you had inherited that gene, you'd be an addict by now. So the taint hasn't attached to you.'

I stared.

'You're free of it.'

'You don't know anything about me,' I said.

He took dainty bites out of his hot pie. 'Point two. Those tattoos on your arms. They can easily be erased. Simply go to a doctor, who will refer you to a surgeon. With new techniques there will be no scars.'

I put my arms under the table.

'Point three. On the question of your mother,' he went on.

'Oh yes?' I gave him a dark look, and took my arms out from under the table.

'You tell me she was a woman who allowed herself to be

overborne. When this Travis pushed her, she gave in. Isn't that true?'

'Yes.'

'Are you like your mother?'

'No. She says I'm like my father. Tough-minded.'

'You need to stop copying her then, and become yourself.'

'Christ,' I exploded.

He smiled. 'Yes. And then there is Christ. The fourth point is that you must take Christ into your life. When you accept that he . . .'

He ran on. I tuned out. I was annoyed, but very much struck by what he'd said.

He ordered extra coffees, sausage rolls and two pieces of cake. He told the girl he would pay when we were done.

'Will you be finishing that pie?' he asked me.

I shook my head.

'Then perhaps I may . . . ?' He ate it in a few efficient mouthfuls. He looked around. The girl who had served us was taking off her apron. A boy came into the shop and they left together.

'Have you got any money?' he asked.

'I've got twenty dollars.'

'We need petrol. And I need to ask you where you're going. I'm going to a settlement in the Far North. I have an errand there, a mission. I serve God, and I have my own private cross to bear. There's been sorrow in my family life, my church family – it strengthens me to love and serve Jesus.' He looked sly suddenly. 'Mine is a secret sorrow.'

'You might as well tell me,' I said with a bleak smile. 'I've told you everything.'

'And I've told you that you're free.' He held up his hand. 'Say no more. Think. There is nothing to hold you back.

'Four points. You're free.'

I followed him to the counter.

'Twenty dollars you said?' He nudged me. I gave it to him. He asked the girl, 'Have you got change for a twenty? Two tens?'

She gave him the change. 'God bless,' he said. We walked out, and he gave me ten dollars.

'Take it all,' I said.

'But you've got nothing else.'

'I've got a bank account.'

The girl called, 'What about paying for the extras?'

'Oh, we paid your colleague for those,' he sang out.

'Awesome,' she called, dopey.

He looked around edgily. 'Perhaps we should get on?'

'You didn't pay for the extras,' I whispered.

'They were your share to pay. And the Lord tells me you need a bit of kindness. He has mercy on people who have suffered, and sometimes he likes to give them a little . . . freebie.'

We sped on.

At Mangonui, I felt car sick. Pastor Kyle went into the shop. He came hurrying out, jumped in and drove off fast, unloading his pockets.

'Take these.' He handed me a tube of antacids. 'I assume you're not employed. You mentioned a bank account?'

I said, ashamed, 'I've been getting the dole.'

'You have to cancel it. You must work. The Lord says if we are to serve him, we must honestly toil to help ourselves.'

I was silent.

'Besides, how much do they give you these days?'

I told him.

'Chicken feed!'

He took me to a tiny bach way out at the end of the white

beach. It was a wild, empty, beautiful place on a hill above the dunes. No one could approach without being visible a long way off. The front windows looked out over the rolling surf. He told me he often saw sharks cruising just beyond the breakers. There were islands on the horizon, and the land rolled away up the coast as far as you could see. From the garden there was a view of the swampland behind the beach, reaching as far as the burnt hill. The garden was sheltered by the house and by a windbreak, and he had a healthy, well-tended vegetable patch. He lived here in the summer, when he wasn't giving sermons in evangelical churches, and when he was away a friend borrowed the place and looked after the garden.

He slept in the bedroom, and I had a couch in the sitting room. There'd been a woman in the place at some stage. I found some dowdy dresses and shoes. One day when he was out I found a pile of children's drawings in a drawer, and a letter written in felt pen in a child's big, uneven handwriting. *I like my new toys. I miss my mum. I have fun and go on walks. I play with toys and ride a bike. I have nice things to eat. I do some lessons and do maths and learn to read. What I wish for is to live with my mum again.*

I closed the drawer. I supposed he must have had a grandchild to stay, but the letter was strange. I couldn't quite see how it fitted. It was a sort of report, and an appeal, but to whom? I wondered whether he was up to something, and imagined some scam involving his church and a charity – fake begging letters that purported to be from African orphans, but were actually penned by a diligent Pastor Kyle.

At night I listened to the surf booming down on the shore. I swam in the sea and took long walks, all the way to the burnt hill. I got fit. We fished off the rocks every day, and our diet consisted of fish, tinned food and vegetables from the garden. He didn't drink or smoke. One day he drove me into town and got me to cancel my dole. I took the money out of my account and gave it to him; he thanked me and said, 'Now you are truly free.' We celebrated with a big meal. For such a thin man, he ate an enormous amount.

I met Nathan in town, and started to go out with him. He'd been a senior rugby league player; he was fit and good looking, with a sweet smile. His family – the respectable side, that is – were ingratiating, handsome people who owned a lot of land in the area. Nathan was the lazy youngest brother of eight children, the bad boy of the family. He'd avoided school and never learned a trade like the others, and ended up working in the dump. His family loved him and indulged him; he was a real favourite.

When Pastor Kyle decided he had to go down to Auckland, I didn't want to live in such an isolated place by myself, so I moved into Nathan's little house on the main road. His mate left the dump to work down south. I took his place, and started working there too.

I often thought about Pastor Kyle's advice. First, I wasn't an addict. Second, I could, if I chose, have my tattoos removed. Third, I didn't have my mother's soft, scatterbrained nature, and therefore I should stop behaving like her and become myself. Fourth, the Lord – well, I chose to forget about him.

When I'd first started going out with Nathan I hadn't shaken off my shame and self-disgust. In those aimless, sensuous, idle months with Hemi, a kind of sweet decay had seeped into my soul. Now things were changing. As time went by I felt the old layers falling away and a new self hardening up – my own true personality. I began to be sharp with Nathan, to be bored by him. Sensing the change, he hit out. He was losing something. I knew what was going to happen: he loved me and I was going to hurt him. Those holiday women who stared at me from their cars, at my black eye, and at the glowering tough guy who'd beaten me up, would have had a firm idea who was the victim. But he had a look of bewilderment and dread after we'd been arguing. When I was sitting on the deck after work he would lie down beside me and rest his head on my knee. He clung to me. And I stroked his hair and stared out over the bay, silent, cold, unyielding.

Huru could see I was changing. He was stirring up trouble, whispering in Nathan's ear. Perhaps he wanted Nathan to kill me, just for his own evil entertainment.


After his stint in Auckland, Pastor Kyle came back to his bach at the end of the white beach. I took to driving to the estuary around the coast from his place, and walking the tracks through the bush. He worked in his garden in the mornings, and when I turned up he stopped and put the kettle on, and served up fresh fish and corn cobs for lunch. We ate out in the garden, looking over the beach. Afterwards, we went fishing.

It was another hot day, the bright light striking off the flax. I climbed Pastor Kyle's hill, intending to tell him about my latest row with Nathan. He wasn't in his garden. I went into the house and put the kettle on, then heard him dropping his boots at the back door.

He came in and looked at me steadily from under his pale lashes.

'You have a black eye.' His tone was flat. He looked hot and irritated.

'It's your fault,' I said, smiling.

'What?'

'You told me to become myself. Nathan doesn't like it.'

'Yourself? Oh, I see.' He took out a packet of cigarettes, lit one and eyed me impatiently. He'd never looked at me like that before, as if I were a nuisance.

'I'll come back another day,' I said, and then burst out, 'I didn't know you smoked.'

He didn't take his eyes off me. 'Want one?' he said.

I took one. He lit it. There was a silence. The wind whistled over the iron roof, a fly buzzed against the window, and the sky in the square of the glass glowed an intense, unclouded blue. I saw that Pastor Kyle had not shaved.

'Is something wrong?'

'No,' he said, mechanically. 'I'm going fishing. Want to come?' There was no encouragement in his voice.

'I'll see you later. Nathan's waiting.'

He watched me go. He waved, and I didn't wave back, wanting him to know I was rather hurt.

I turned off the track and lay down under a tree. It was Saturday, and since I didn't have anything to do I thought I might turn back and have a swim at the white beach. I lay in the shade, looking up at the sky through the leaves, too lazy to move. After half an hour I heard someone on the track. I saw Pastor Kyle walking quickly, carrying a pack on his back and a large box in his arms. The box was criss-crossed all over with blue and black packing tape.

I lay in the scrub, waiting until he was a distance off, still visible through the trees. I followed. He left the track that led to the coastal settlement and turned down a steep slope. He disappeared from view. I hurried to an outcrop of rock and looked down. He was making his way through the trees to a sandy path that followed the coast just above the rocks.

I sat on the rock. The sun blazed down, and the sea glittered. The sandy path he'd taken must lead round the coast to the jetty where I'd left Nathan's car. I decided to follow him, and if he caught me, to say that I'd seen him come down that way and thought it might be a good shortcut. The only thing that made me hesitate was his expression as he'd passed me. There was something so fixed, so coldly intent in it, that I didn't like the thought of getting in his way.

I skidded down the slope and onto the path, which wound between rocks, under clay banks and over tangled pohutukawa roots. Below, the dark blue sea, deep here, washed in among the rocks, and further out gannets circled and swooped and dive-bombed, surfacing with fish in their beaks. The hot wind flipped the shiny leaves and the pohutukawa flowers blazed red against the sky. There was the iridescent sheen in the air that you get on very hot days. I passed under trees laden with straw bundles of gannets' nests, the birds clacking their beaks and shitting down onto the white-streaked rocks, the air pungent with the smell of fish. I was heading out onto a small peninsula. The path went around an outcrop and then there was no more path; just white sand and a long, lonely, beautiful stretch of coast fringed with bush, out of sight of the jetty, which lay behind the curve of the land, inside the estuary.

Pastor Kyle had walked in the hard sand near the water. His footprints were visible. Where the beach met the trees the sand was smooth and cool, and behind the small dunes the bush made a thick, sheltering canopy. The sand was bone-white and the estuary water was very clear, with a fast current in it. The tide was going out, the water running between the shore and an island. I stuck close to the edge of the bush, following the footprints until they crossed the beach and entered the forest. Near the shore I came to a sunny clearing in the trees.

There was a tiny weatherboard house, a boat pulled up on the sand below it, and a long fishing line strung out on poles into the estuary. Beside the house, in a clearing striped with sunlight, the air warm and still and dusty, was a wooden picnic table, at which a fat woman was reading a book. A small boy in yellow togs decorated with skulls and crossbones waded out of the water and ran towards her, cannoning into her side; she dropped her book and pushed him away, saying in a lazy, good-natured voice, 'Get off, you, you're soaking wet.'

I watched them. The boy lay down under the long line and covered himself with sand. The woman went back to her book. I decided to walk past them along the shore. I turned, and Pastor Kyle was standing behind me.

He was holding a bucket. In it was a mess of scraps and bones and blood.

'I followed you,' I said.

'I see that.' His gaze was steady.

'I thought it would be a shortcut to the car.'

'I'm going to feed the pig,' he said. 'Come with me.'

I followed him into the clearing.

'This is Mrs Sendells,' he said. The woman closed her book and sat back. She had a massive face and forehead, large eyes, wiry, curly hair and a small, thin-lipped, ugly mouth. Her eyes were grey. She looked at me expressionlessly, her massive arms folded. The boy came trailing over, covered in sand, and leaned against her. He was about seven years old, with close-cropped brown hair and freckles on his nose.

'This is Joseph.' Pastor Kyle patted the boy's head. The boy smiled shyly and looked away.

'I'll show you the track back,' Pastor Kyle told me, and walked off.

'Nice to meet you,' I said to the woman.

'God bless,' she said. Her eyes followed me. Her expression didn't change.

I hurried after Pastor Kyle. A short distance from the house was a smelly enclosure made of wooden boards. The pig stuck its hairy snout through a gap, grunting and squealing. Pastor Kyle emptied the slops.

'She's your wife?'

He sighed and put down the bucket. 'Mrs Sendells usually lives in Auckland. She's having a holiday. There's no room in my little shack.'

'Who's the boy?'

'A member of my church.' He faced me. 'Any other questions?'

'No. Only you never mentioned . . .'

'You've stayed in my house. That doesn't mean you're part of my family.' His eyes were cold.

'No.' I looked away, stung.

'I'll show you the track.'

He led me up a slope to a headland above the beach. We climbed across rocks, crashed through a bit of bush and came to a track that led to the jetty where I'd left the car.

I set off but he called me back.

'Angela. I've helped you, haven't I? You've stayed in my house. We're . . . friends.'

'Yes.'

'I should explain. There are issues in our church family . . . A young woman, one of our community, had a divorce that, well, it was very sad. She's needed a refuge for her son, Joseph. Mrs Sendells and I have agreed to help.'

'A young woman . . . ?'

'Yes, it's a bad domestic situation. There's a difficult, violent, cunning ex-husband, who mustn't find out where his son is. Young Joseph needs safety and privacy. Do you understand?'

'I won't tell anyone.'

'Absolute privacy.'

'I understand.'

'God bless you,' he said.

I drove home, thinking it over. A woman had got Pastor Kyle to hide her son from his father. I remembered the letter in a child's handwriting that I'd found in Pastor Kyle's drawer. The letter had said, 'What I wish for is to live with my mum.' Who was the letter addressed to? It was all very strange. I went round and round it and didn't know what to think.

Nathan was in a better mood when I got home and I forgot about Pastor Kyle. But I woke in the night and thought of it again. Pastor Kyle's manner had been odd, strained. And yet there could be a perfectly good explanation. In any case, he was right. I owed him, and I would have to mind my own business.

A fortnight later I came home from the dump, turned on the TV and there was a picture of the boy I'd seen, on the six o'clock news.

*

Nathan had mates over. They were rowdily drinking beer. One of the cousins, picking at a guitar, broke into scraps of melody that were strikingly sweet and true. They were crowded into the sitting room and I couldn't shut them up, nor watch the late news. The little party went on for longer than I could endure. I lay in bed seething with frustration. At four in the morning a string broke on the guitar, there was a brief spat followed by reunion: loud oaths of allegiance hoarsely sworn under the bedroom window, under a bone-white slice of summer moon. I lifted the blind and saw a speckled streak of moonlight glittering across the bay. Four battered utes roared into life and the cousins sped off. Nathan came scraping his way along the hallway wall, towards bed.

The next day I went straight to the shop for a paper. The story was on the front page. It was a child custody battle that had taken a striking turn. Pastor Kyle had lied: the boy's name wasn't Joseph, it was Samir Jarrar. According to the paper, the boy's mother, one Karen Lot, had been accused of serious child neglect. The Family Court had taken the boy from her and awarded full custody to the father, Ramzi Jarrar, who was a Lebanese New Zealander, a pharmacist. Karen Lot, the article said, had then colluded in a plan with her father, a Mr Bryan Lot, to kidnap the child and hide him away from Mr Jarrar, in defiance of the court order. Bryan Lot had abducted the boy and disappeared, and Karen Lot was refusing to say where he and the boy were. Mr Jarrar was appealing for information. The police were searching for the boy. How had Pastor Kyle and his wife ended up with the child? The only clue was that Bryan Lot was a pastor in an evangelical church.

In a side article I found this: *Letters have been received, purporting to be from the child, Samir Jarrar, saying that he is well and happy, and asking that he be allowed to live with his mother, not his father. The authenticity of these letters has been questioned by the boy's father, Ramzi Jarrar, who says his son, aged six, does not have the skill to write them.*

Pastor Kyle and his wife must have agreed with the Lots that they would take the boy and hide him from Mr Jarrar. But the Family Court had decided Karen Lot wasn't a fit parent and that Mr Jarrar was. Surely the court would know best?

I drove back to the estuary that afternoon. I parked the car back from the road in a lay-by where I hoped it wouldn't be seen. I walked past the jetty, along the track, over the rocks and down the slope through the trees.

I hid and watched. There was no sign of life. I went further into the clearing. The house was empty. The windows were closed, the door was locked and the long line had been reeled in. The pig was gone from its pen.

I walked along the shore. The tide was sluicing out towards the mouth of the estuary. Shadows slanted across the beach. I walked around the curve of coast until I came to the sandy path. I set out, with the uneasy fear that someone might be watching me from the hillside above. I hurried past the gannets' nests, round the rocks. There was rain out at sea, great curtains of water sweeping in, and the sea had a metallic sheen. A shower dripped down through the branches and the wind sighed in the treetops. I reached the bottom of the hill below Pastor Kyle's bach. Instead of going up the path I clambered through the scrub, and arrived on a section of bank behind his house, looking down on the garden. There was no sign of him or his wife or the boy. I stayed in my perch for a long time, until the shadows grew long and spiky on the dunes, and the thought of darkness began to bother me. I left my lookout and retraced my steps.

I drove home. The house I'd seen a month ago seemed remote now. Perhaps the boy in the clearing wasn't the one pictured on the news. The fat woman with her ugly, curly mouth and her level stare, the little boy covered in sand, Pastor Kyle with his bucket of bones; the scene took on the flavour of a fairy tale or dream, touched with faint, sensual menace: the golden, dusty light among the trees, sunshine and shadow, the murmur of the sea.

Nathan was sitting on the deck rolling a beer can over his forehead. I sat down beside him. 'Nathan, don't tell anyone this. Promise?'

He shrugged. Nodded.

'I've seen that boy. Samir Jarrar, the one in the news whose grandfather kidnapped him.'

He didn't say anything. He stopped rolling the can over his face.

'You know the one I mean?'

'Yes,' he said.

'I saw him.'

'Where?'

'In a house over at the estuary. Only he's gone now.'

'They said on TV that boy is in Taupo.'

'Well, he's not,' I said, looking sharply at him. I was surprised he knew what I was talking about. 'I only saw him once, but it was him all right.'

He stood up. 'I don't believe it.'

I threw up my hands.

He said quietly, 'Are you trying to stir up trouble?'

'No.'

'Do you know how many police would come crashing through here if you spread this?'

'No.'

'Then maybe you should keep your mouth shut.'

I said slowly, 'Pastor Kyle's got him. It was his house.'

'Pastor Kyle? He's your friend. He's everyone's friend up

here. If you get him into trouble, for no reason . . .' He put his arms around me. 'Don't make trouble. We have to live here. I love you. Do you know how much I love you?'

I pushed him away impatiently. Hurt flashed in his eyes. I leaned against him, and he held me tight, pushing his face into my shoulder. We sat like that, in silence, while the last of the sunset lit up the hillside and the shadows darkened in the dips and gullies above the bay.

Days went by. We worked in the dump. The weather grew cooler and the settlement emptied out. Now there were days of rain, soaking the brown land, making rivers of red mud at the sides of the roads. The bay was calm and still, the water silvery. We fished from the rocks in the early mornings, in the salty silence under the pohutukawa trees. Stingrays glided under the water, rippling their wings, fish jumped, rain dimpled the water. Nathan slid off the rocks with a mask and snorkel, gathering kina, diving and surfacing like a seal. Under the white sky, ringed by black, wet rocks, the bay seemed to be holding itself in check. All was calm, the only sound was the patter of the rain.

One afternoon Nathan gathered a sack of kina and loaded it into the ute. We drove along the dirt road towards the pine forest. There was mist hanging over the tops, the camping ground was deserted, and in the forest the air was cool and damp. We both shivered at once, and looked at one another and laughed. Once we got stuck and Nathan had to rock the ute backwards and forwards, until we shot out of it with a roar and a spray of mud.

Huru came across the clearing to meet us, taking the sack of kina. Three women brought chairs onto the deck and began to take the innards out of the kina with spoons. The children tottered around, the toddlers wearing only nappies, despite the chill. Huru took Nathan aside and talked in his ear. Nathan nodded and chewed his nails, and occasionally broke out in a false little chuckle. They walked away into the trees.

Mereana offered me a spoon for the kina. There was a lot of clutter on the deck, clothes hanging on lines above our heads, stacked tools, a yard broom. I looked at a pair of boy's yellow swimming togs, decorated with skulls and crossbones.

I spooned out the messy kina and tipped it into a bowl. One of the women started singing, low and tuneful and sweet.

'Seen Pastor Kyle lately?' I asked Mereana.

She rolled her eyes and smacked her lips and laughed, 'Oh, he never comes out here. No never. He doesn't come here.' She grinned at me, toothless, shaking her head. 'Not him, oh no.' The rain drifted against the dark wall of the trees. Mereana offered me a beer. We worked, listening to the low singing. Mereana looked at me again, chuckling and shaking her head. Her eyes were very bright. I put my hand on her arm. 'I'll just go to the toilet.'

I went quickly through the musty bedroom; there was nothing but the bed and a pile of clothes. In the lean-to laundry, under a pile of coats, I found a large box striped with black and blue tape – the box I'd seen Pastor Kyle carry from his bach.

Outside, Huru and Nathan were shaking hands. We left, driving out as the last patches of light were gleaming in the sky. I pretended to have a headache, and went to bed as soon as we got home.

At first light next morning I took the ute. On Pastor Kyle's track the bush sparkled with dew and the ground sent up a wet, earthy scent. The surf was rough at the white beach, the waves booming. I knocked on Pastor Kyle's door. He opened it, wearing pyjama trousers and a holey grey jersey. The place smelled of cigarette smoke.

I walked in and said, 'You've given that boy to Huru.'

He stood very still. He lit a cigarette, never taking his eyes off me.

'Sit down,' he said.

Slowly, he went to the kettle and filled it. He cleared his throat. 'You're upset. You don't know what you're talking about.'

'The police are looking for him. If you don't send him back I'm going to tell someone.'

He faced me. 'Angela. Think about what you're saying. You want to make trouble for your friends?'

'I won't get anyone into trouble if you send him home.'

'Home?'

'He's supposed to be with his father. He's got a custody order. You can't leave him out there.'

'You will let me down. And others.' He pursed his lips, studied his fingernails, considering. 'You might like to think about this. Nathan drove the boy out there. He's involved in this. And so are you, that means.'

He looked at me steadily. There was a silence.

'I don't care,' I said.

'Think. You had nothing before you came here. This is your home, your community. Huru . . .'

'How can you have anything to do with Huru?'

'Huru understands what's right. That boy was being brought up without his church family. Without God.'

'And he's with God now? That place is evil. If you leave him there, you're evil.'

'You're going to betray Nathan,' he said.

He paused, and then added softly, 'What will Huru think about that?'

I snatched up one of his cigarettes and lit it. My hand trembled. 'If you don't send him back in three days, I'll ring the police.'

He put the kettle carefully down. 'Is this the new self, the new you?'

'I'll give you three days,' I repeated.

His expression was dreamy, strange. He mouthed a couple of words, smiled, shook his head and said, 'I took you in.'

I faltered, 'That's not the point . . .'

He came towards me, his voice toneless, mechanical. 'You're faithless. Disloyal. You are the slut daughter of a drug-addicted whore.'

I ran out and fled down the path. I stopped on the track several times, fearing he was following me. Panicking, I couldn't start the engine; finally I got it going and drove towards home.

I pulled over on our road and looked at Nathan's little house with the beautiful, misty bay spread out before it, the water crossed by cloud shadows, the gannets circling and plummeting, hitting the water like bombs. A squall disturbed the calm; the water broke into a million glittering ripples. Pastor Kyle was right; I couldn't go home. This was the last time I would sit here, looking over the bay.

I turned the ute around and headed for the main road. The sun was rising higher over the baked brown hills; the eastern sky was pink, the light glowed softly at the edges of the clouds. A hawk flew up from the road and circled lazily away. A feeling rose in me, so reckless, so happy . . . I nearly drove myself off the road.

I made it to Auckland in the evening and found a room in a cheap motel in Greenlane. I abandoned Nathan's ute in a car park. I waited. Pastor Kyle was cunning, and he wouldn't want trouble. He would know I was serious about telling someone. Sure enough, after three days, the TV news reported that the boy had turned up at a small police station outside Whangarei. He was returned to his father.

The following month it was reported that Nathan and Huru had been arrested in the settlement. There were drug charges. They were to be questioned about Samir Jarrar. Pastor Kyle's name wasn't mentioned; his role in the affair stayed a secret between him and his God. As far as I know he's managed to keep it that way. No one talks to the police up there.

I have no God to reproach me for the hurt I've caused. To Nathan, I mean. If this were a story, I would dedicate it to him. To Nathan John Hetaraka.

Two weeks after I got back to Auckland I'd found a job in a restaurant and a room in a flat. I was working hard, earning good tips, preparing for the operation to remove my tattoos.

# DAVE ARMSTRONG

Wellington writer Dave Armstrong has written extensively for screen and stage – as well as a few speeches. He won Best New New Zealand Play in two consecutive years at the Chapman Tripp Theatre Awards for *The Tutor* and *Niu Sila* (co-written with Oscar Kightley). His musical play *King and Country* has been performed throughout the country and on radio. Armstrong's television credits include *Seven Periods with Mr Gormsby*, *Bro'town*, *The Semisis*, *Skitz* and *Shortland Street*. He won an AFTA television award for Best Comedy Script for *Spin Doctors*. He has written one book, *True Colours*, about the 1996 general election, and is currently Writer in Residence at Victoria University.

# FOODBANQUET

After the stunning success of multimillionaire Horton Boner's fiftieth birthday party, Janet Stanton insisted that she and her husband David, Chief Political Adviser to the Prime Minister, host a dinner party in their Eastbourne villa. Of course, the Stantons didn't have the money of the Boners, but what they lacked in dollars they made up in class.

Le Grand Boeuf, as David Stanton described it, was to be a five course degustation meal. It would use the freshest and highest quality local ingredients and be accompanied by some superb New Zealand wines.

As soon as the guests arrived, they sat in the lounge with

a glass of champagne and some crudités, and admired not only David Stanton's large collection of books, but also the Stantons' many works of New Zealand art. There were arty Albrechts, fashionable Fomisons, a frisky Frizzell, a chaotic Clairmont and a humorous Hammond that David sold his car – a Fiat Bambina – to purchase just after he and Janet were married. The highlight of their art collection sat opposite the prime piece of real estate – their large plate glass window, which afforded such a superb view of Wellington Harbour. And what better work to have as the centrepiece of your private art collection than a landscape painting by Colin McCahon? Privately, both David and Janet detested The McCahon – Janet thought that the hills didn't seem real – but you couldn't own a McCahon and not display it.

While Janet was given a free hand in decor for their villa, David insisted he have a say on the purchase of art. After all, as well as being the Prime Minister's Chief Political Adviser, David was also a novelist (unpublished), photographer, portraitist, essayist, composer, playwright, art critic, curator, and collector of objets d'art. While some commentators called him a jack of all trades, he described himself as a Renaissance man. Just talking about the price of his art collection gave him countless hours of intense pleasure.

Above the white Steinway and the white miniature bust of Picasso (the painter, not the Stantons' dog) was a batik by Hamish Delahunty, *Waihi 1912*, which celebrated the famous miners' strike. The blood-red of Delahunty's banners contrasted nicely with the aquamarine tint of Stanton's framed citation from the International Monetary Fund praising his excellence in promoting the government's deregulation of the labour market. Thanks to the employment regulations introduced by the government of Norman Kinghorn, strikes were now a thing of the past. The only downside of this, as far as David Stanton was concerned, was that there would be no more epic labour strikes in the country, so no more Hamish Delahunty batiks celebrating them, which was a great pity. Then again, Stanton could hardly persuade his boss to repeal some of the country's most important legislation since the 1930s just so he could have a batik to match his existing one. While Stanton fully supported Kinghorn's industrial legislation, it didn't exactly produce great art. Stanton couldn't see how you could create an interesting batik out of seven Samoan cleaners grumpily signing a 'take it or leave it' contract from a large American multinational – unless of course the female cleaners were particularly large. He briefly considered persuading the Arts Council to fund and organise a strike somewhere – for purely visual purposes – and then invite Delahunty along to make a batik work of it, but decided against it.

There was an air of expectancy in the lounge – Janet Stanton's dinner parties were legendary. Earlier in the year had been the wildly popular Rude Food evening. It was a great success despite the fact that one of the guests was allergic to cucumbers and guava, and another to seaweed. Tonight, everyone was expecting something even better, but before Janet revealed her latest culinary surprise, David Stanton insisted that the guests play one of his favourite pre-dinner games – guessing the opera. They all listened as the music boomed out through the tiny yet powerful speakers.

'It's obviously Italian,' announced Horton Boner's wife, Paloma. 'I'll guess Puccini.'

'Bellissimo,' screeched David Stanton in a high soprano, with his hand over the cover of the CD so no one could see the title of the opera, 'but which one?'

'I saw *Madam Butterfly* and *Manon Lescaut* in Europe recently, I'd know if it was either of them,' commented Horton Boner authoritatively, 'and I caught *Turandot* while I was on an art-buying trip to Australia. I'll guess it's either the finale of *Tosca*, or the Act Two finale of *Bohème*.'

The Maori novelist and newly appointed member of Kinghorn's thinktank, Earl Tipene Mountbatten, who was sitting by the bar enjoying a Campari, smirked.

'Au contraire,' interjected Tipene smugly. 'Would anyone mind if I hazard a guess?'

'Of course not, Tipene,' said Paloma warmly, delighted to see a Maori who was interested in the vastly superior culture of the West. 'I didn't realise you had such a love of . . . "our" culture.'

'Oh yes,' replied the novelist. 'I may have grown up in Broad Range, one of the worst suburbs in our town, yet when I was eight I got a job delivering newspapers every morning from six until eight. On the first week I got paid, I gave half of the money to my mother to pay for groceries, and with the other I bought a recording of Telemann's trio sonatas on original instruments.'

The guests were most impressed – they had a cultured and educated Maori in their midst. Not a Bad Maori but a Good Maori, and everyone so loved a Good Maori.

'Come on, Tip,' encouraged Boner, 'guess away. I'm sure you can do it.'

Before Tipene spoke, he thoughtfully cleared his throat for a few seconds. He had learnt this style of oratory by observing Maori elders speaking on the marae – on the few occasions he had visited. The throat-clearing, part of Maoridom's rich oral tradition, implied that the speaker had humility and grace, and was fully aware of the mana of the occasion at which he was speaking – and it was always a 'he' on a marae.

Tipene thought that the throat-clearing, like most Maori oral traditions, was total rubbish – it just made the speaker sound like he was badly in need of a few drops of cough medicine. But what did impress Tipene was the incredible effect the stunt had on Pakehas. Just because you had a brown face, hoiked a bit and paused before speaking, they immediately assumed that what you were going to say was extremely profound. Little did these Pakehas know that the real reason Tipene inserted these extended gaps of silence whenever he was speaking in public was that he was buying time – using the pauses to think of what in the hell he could say next. After the last throat-clear, Tipene made his guess.

'*Gianni Schicchi*,' said Tipene nervously, 'just before Zita furiously tells Rinuccio never to speak to her again of Gianni Schicchi.' The Maori novelist then added ever so smugly: 'Felicity Palmer playing Zita, Roberto Alagna playing Rinuccio, with the London Symphony Orchestra conducted by Anthony Pappano. EMI Classics CDS5 56587-2.'

Everyone sat in awestruck silence – this Maori really knew his stuff.

'That's just a wild guess, of course,' added Tipene modestly, and placed his empty glass back on the bar. He could hear Prime Minister Norman Kinghorn asking Horton Boner, in a loud whisper, if Tipene was related to the great Kiri Te Kanawa.

'Very good,' replied David Stanton as he scrupulously checked the CD cover. 'Just one detail to clear up to win the bottle of Moët.'

In order to show off his excellent French pronunciation, Stanton left the 't' off 'Moët', not realising that since the champagne maker's name was originally Dutch (Mr Chandon was French, but Mr Moët was Dutch), the 't' in Moët was hard.

'Sure,' answered Earl Tipene Mountbatten, confident he could answer any question about *Gianni Schicchi* that Stanton could dream up.

'How many p's in the name of the conductor, Anthony Pappano?'

'Oh, that's so easy,' laughed Paloma Boner. 'Tony's such a dear, you know. Horton and I had a candlelit supper with him one night at Convent Garden.'

Tipene froze, and was in such shock he didn't even bother correcting Paloma's 'convent' to 'covent'. The trouble was that he couldn't remember how to spell the conductor's name. It would come eventually, but he had to play for time. He cleared his throat yet again. He could spell the name of every vocal Maori activist dependent on welfare – and there were thousands of them; he could spell the name of every cringey, Pakeha, kaftan-wearing, liberal educationist that called him racist for his views on Maoris – and it seemed like there were millions of them too; but he could not remember how to spell the name of a single opera conductor.

Tipene coughed once more and made up some Maori-sounding gibberish while he went into a trance-like state. Paloma Boner authoritatively informed everyone that Tipene was communicating with his ancestors – Maoris did that sort of thing apparently.

Tipene didn't really care whether or not he won a bottle of Moët – he'd seen too many Maori families destroyed by alcohol to covet it – but the most important thing was that he didn't want to make a fool of himself in front of all these educated Pakehas. Only last Monday, he'd written a newspaper column lambasting the appalling literacy standards of bookless Maoris. Luckily his word processor had a spell-check, which meant no one ever knew about his hidden weakness – Tipene was a truly dreadful speller. In fact, even as he wrote the article on literacy, Tipene had to consult a dictionary, as the spell-check did not know the correct spelling of the word 'spell-check' and Tipene didn't know if the word spell-check was spelt 'spellcheck', 'spell check' or 'spell-check'.

Tipene decided that the minute he got home, he would enter the name of Anthony Pappano and all the other world-famous opera conductors into the spell-check on his computer.

The Maori novelist had done everything he could to learn to spell, but those bookless years growing up in a poor subdivision on the outskirts of a North Island provincial town had taken their toll. No matter how many classes he attended or remedial language tapes he purchased, he just couldn't master the art of spelling. Tipene silently cursed his bookless parents for allowing him to spend his youth fishing, playing, singing and dancing when he should have been inside at his desk (he never had a desk until he was thirty-one) learning to spell.

Tipene could stall no longer. He realised his Pakeha friends would discover his weakness – a disability he had never mentioned when he made his aggressive and arrogant pronouncements about the strength of the individual, the importance of enterprise and the need for Maoris to throw off the shackles of welfare dependency and embrace technology such as computers, email and spell-checkers.

'Two p's,' replied Tipene, in an embarrassed manner that made his answer sound like a question, 'one at the front and one in the middle.'

The guests all exploded with laughter.

'Pappano with one p at the front?' giggled Horton.

'Who'd ever have thought?' chortled Paloma. 'I must email him and tell him we've changed his name. Tony would love that.'

Tipene sat mortified as the laughter continued.

'Looks like the Moët's still up for grabs,' announced David Stanton.

As the conversation moved on to visual arts, Tipene decided to keep his mouth shut for the remainder of the evening – he didn't want all the Pakehas finding out he was colour-blind as well.

Gretchen van der Flanders was mightily relieved that Tipene was now a laughing stock – it would save her from having to make an extremely embarrassing apology. When Gretchen arrived, Janet Stanton had forgotten to introduce the van der Flanders to all the guests. Gretchen's husband, Eddie, was a Religious Studies lecturer and, like Earl Tipene Mountbatten and David Stanton, a member of the Prime Minister's thinktank. When he arrived, Eddie asked his wife if she wouldn't mind fixing him a drink, then went straight to the bookshelf in the lounge to browse through *The Impressionist Nude*, a large art book which stood on the bookshelf next to an extremely well-thumbed volume entitled *The Obese Nude through the Ages*.

Gretchen had arrived at the bar to find a tall Maori stranger standing behind it, fixing a Campari. Gretchen naturally assumed that Janet had hired a barman. After all, he was a Maori, he was wearing a tuxedo, and it was becoming very fashionable in Wellington society to hire home help, especially since Norman Kinghorn's recently introduced employment legislation had made it possible to hire servants without the problems of penal rates, holiday pay, compulsory union membership and overtime. Rather than greet Tipene, Gretchen simply addressed him the way she spoke to all her bar staff at Konditerei Hitler.

'Bacardi and Coke, small glass, and go easy on the ice,' she demanded frostily.

Tipene was a little surprised by her manner, but said nothing, as he was feeling particularly privileged to be amongst such cultured, educated people who owned many, many books – even if they didn't necessarily read them. He smilingly presented Gretchen with a very nice Bacardi and Coke – a drink he had become expert in making for molls at various gang parties during his bookless, antisocial adolescence in various North Island provincial towns. Gretchen noticed there was rather a large amount of ice in the glass.

'I said go easy on the ice, you stupid prick.'

Tipene, not wanting to offend the Nordic beauty, quickly grabbed some of the ice cubes out of her glass.

'Get those dirty brown hands out of my glass or I'll kick you in the balls.'

Gretchen had learnt over the years that one needed to be particularly firm with hired help, especially if it was brown. Tipene apologised and obediently made a fresh Bacardi and Coke – with far less ice. When he'd finished, Gretchen didn't thank him, but simply snatched the glass. Despite the woman's extreme rudeness, Tipene thought he should introduce himself to her. Although Gretchen had acted like she didn't know him, Tipene suspected she was simply adopting this haughty tone because she was in awe of being in the company of a great novelist. Surely she had read the countless magazine articles about him, or seen him on the television commenting on Maori issues? Tipene gave a friendly smile and extended his hand.

'Tipene,' he said, warmly and quietly, so as to leave no doubt that although a great writer and a possible Nobel Prize winner one day, in real life he was just like any normal, everyday Maori who'd cast off the shackles of welfarism and achieved excellence. Gretchen glowered at him.

'Tip you? You've got a cheek.'

She fumbled around in her expensive black handbag, found two coins, and slammed them into the writer's extended hand.

'You Maoris certainly know what side your kumara bread is buttered on, don't you? Doing an undeclared cash job like this – I bet you're probably getting some sort of benefit from Ngati Welfare, not to mention collecting all the seafood you want with your special privileges for anything that grows or swims in this country. And then you have the audacity to ask for tips. I've got a mind to call up WINZ and dob you in. Mind you, you're probably paying maintenance to some poor bitch and two bastard niggerlings, so it would only end up hurting the little piccaninnies. Comprendez?'

Though her words were insulting, Tipene couldn't help but be strangely attracted to this strapping blonde. There was nothing he liked more than an assertive northern European. She reminded him of an Aeroflot air hostess. Though he associated the airline with communist inefficiency, he always liked the flight attendants. Gretchen was strong, astute and possessed considerable business acumen. If only the Maoris could produce women like that, he thought.

'So you speak French?' said Tipene, most impressed. 'It's a lovely language. My children have their own private tutor –

Pascal. She's an exchange student from Montpellier – the kids love her.'

Gretchen made an upward gesture with her middle finger at the writer. Tipene couldn't help but notice what lovely hands she had – enhanced by a beautiful gold ring on her middle finger, studded with South African diamonds. On the finger next to the ring was a solitary gold wedding band. Whoever was married to this woman, thought Tipene, was a very lucky man. But before Tipene could say a word, Gretchen left to find Janet Stanton, so she could complain to her host about her terrible brown help.

Horton Boner was eventually awarded the bottle of Moët, as he spelt Pappano correctly. Boner didn't really care for opera, though he liked ones set in the seventeenth and eighteenth centuries as they often had duels in them with quite wonderful pistols.

'I could take this Moët home with me,' grinned Boner, 'but since I'm a good socialist, or at least I was in my youth, I think I'll share it around. Whoever's on the lowest income gets the most!'

Everyone laughed as he popped open the bottle.

'And if we want to buy another bottle,' added Kinghorn good-naturedly, 'I'd only have to cut benefits by one dollar per person per week, and we'd have enough to keep us going all year.'

The gathering roared, so heartily sick were they of hearing wet economists advocate that adding just one dollar per person in tax per week would raise money for some hospital or school or cancer-screening facility. It was nice to hear someone do it the other way around – even if he was only joking.

Gretchen was now feeling very guilty so went over to Tipene to apologise.

'Dearest Tipene,' she said, 'I made a big gaffe earlier this evening.'

'That's great,' replied the author. 'I've got some enterprising cousins in the Bay of Plenty who run a tourism venture for Japanese tourists – I'm sure they'd be happy to have us come along.'

Tipene assumed Norman Kinghorn must have told her about the Maoris' love of night-time eeling, but before Gretchen could reply, David Stanton rang the gong for dinner.

Stanton had selected a gong in concert A, in keeping with the operatic theme of the early part of the evening, and he tapped it in the rhythm of the opening bars of *Gianni Schicchi* as he called them to dinner – though Tipene was the only one who noticed.

Janet and the real brown help – a large Samoan woman called Maria, whom Janet's husband had met while she was cleaning the Beehive – heaved the first course of Le Grand Boeuf onto the table. Janet lifted the lid off the large tray with a virtuoso flourish. The assembled guests gasped, then applauded loudly.

The tripe was sautéed with onions, then mixed with a bread stuffing and flavoured with traditional parsley, sage and thyme. Peach juice was added and then the entire dish was seared very quickly over a natural fire – the same fire that famous performance artist Tegel Giblett had pissed in earlier – which gave the tripe a subtle acidic flavour throughout, not unlike Vietnamese mint, which was actually a member of the coriander family despite its name.

Though tripe was actually very cheap to buy nowadays, the

assembled moneyed guests knew that offal dishes were classy. By contrast, Janet's usual favourites such as Beef Wellington, lamb fillet with tamarillo, lamb shanks or orange roughy with juniper berries, while quite pricey, were no longer considered fashionable. Nothing could compete with simple offal.

David uncorked a cheeky gewürztraminer and an introverted though enigmatic Hawke's Bay sauvignon blanc, and decided on Alban Berg's *Lyric Suite* as the perfect accompanying music for a load of tripe.

The tripe was delicious and the next dish just as impressive. The thinly sliced lamb's fry was marinated Middle Eastern-style in lemon juice, onion and cinnamon, then pan-fried in some sort of alcohol, before being laid to rest on a 'gravestone' of Creole cornbread, and accompanied by a puha salsa. This novel mixture of cuisines greatly impressed the guests, and all agreed that the possibilities for more cross-cultural fusion – hangi-cooked tortillas stuffed with eel, kina enchiladas, paua tostadas, boiled cabbage with corn chips – were endless.

The *Lyric Suite* ended, so to keep the music matched with the cuisine, Stanton chose to play a recently released CD of songs by Maori nose-flute specialist Joe Punakaiki, the brother of Hera Punakaiki, the famous Greymouth Maori glass-blower and illustrator of Tipene's first novel. While David Stanton loved Punakaiki's rendition of Elton John's 'Song for Guy', his wife's particular favourite was Joe's arrangement of 'Memory' from *Cats*.

The guests enthused about the lamb's fry, but no one could guess what alcohol it was fried in. Paloma suggested that it was a dry vermouth, while Gretchen suspected brandy.

Next came poached baby paua on a bed of spinach, with a terrine of pipi and mussel. The guests agreed this dish was absolutely divine, and were it not for the incredible chicken cooked with pomegranate and walnut sauce that followed, they would have happily finished their meal with the paua.

The final course was the dessert – twelve individually made sorbets, each one a different colour. The lightness of the ice and the delicately sweet fruit flavour was just what was required after the large main course. The sorbet flavours included passionfruit, mango, pawpaw and grapefruit, and David provided everyone with a sweet though slightly self-effacing sauternes from the Bay of Plenty to accompany the Torbay Sorbet – named in honour of Janet Stanton's Aunt Lois who was the Treasurer for the Torbay branch of the East Coast Bays National Party and who taught Janet how to cook.

David chose a gigue from Bach's *Goldberg Variations* to accompany this course, which caused the Boners to complain, as Stanton's recording was on piano, not the original harpsichord. Horton likened Bach on a piano to a dessert with artificial colouring and flavouring, but Stanton defended his recording.

'This is not just any old pianist,' said David gleefully, 'but the great Glenn Gould.'

'Your point being?' wondered Horton.

'He's internationally famous for playing Bach on the piano.'

This was not good enough for the Boners, who'd never heard of Glenn Gould. Tipene agreed with his good friends and patrons.

'There are some things,' said Tipene, after clearing his throat a number of times, 'on which my people and I have to stand tall – tu tangata – and Bach being performed on original instruments is one of them. Ake, ake, ake.'

Janet defused the tense situation by putting her most prized possession, a CD of *The Phantom of the Opera* autographed by the great Andrew Lloyd Webber himself, into the CD player. That caused no problem with anyone, once Janet had assured Tipene and the Boners that it was indeed the authentic original cast recording of the musical.

As David Stanton passed around the port, everyone showered fulsome praise on Janet's wonderful banquet. The Stantons had truly shown that when it came to putting on a good social occasion, money wasn't everything. While David had absolutely no interest in his wife in the bedroom, he was extremely proud of her ability in the kitchen.

'Janet is an absolute marvel when it comes to cooking,' he skited. 'Throw her a foodbank parcel and she could make a five course banquet for twelve out of it.'

Janet couldn't help blushing.

'That's exactly what I did, darling.'

'Come on,' said Kinghorn, as he patted his large stomach, 'that food was delicious, you wouldn't get all that from a foodbank. I hope not, anyway, otherwise I'll be cutting the amount of government funding they receive.'

'We don't give them a bean, anyway,' giggled David Stanton. 'They're mainly run by the churches.'

'Believe it or not, almost a hundred per cent of this meal comes from a foodbank,' announced Janet.

The fascinated guests realised she was not kidding.

'You see,' explained Janet, 'Paloma and I had a little bet.'

'It's all part of a game we play in Parnell,' blurted out Horton's wife, excited, 'between the ski season and the yachting season.'

'It's called Foodbanquet,' reported Janet.

Paloma Boner outlined the rules: 'Each player must dress up in a disguise, such as tatty old op-shop clothes, go to the nearest foodbank, which is quite a long way if you live in Parnell, and apply for a food parcel. Using only the contents of the foodbank parcel, you must prepare a banquet for twelve, or more correctly a Foodbanquet – which is what Janet did tonight.'

'Very successfully, I'd say,' added a laughing Horton Boner, who hadn't been in on the joke.

'Of course,' giggled Janet, 'it can be quite hard actually obtaining a foodbank parcel, as they try to only give them to the genuinely needy. But that's half the fun of the game.'

Norman Kinghorn roared with laughter. 'It sounds like great fun.'

'You have to be quite clever to outwit them,' continued Janet. 'You have to lie about your personal circumstances, make up false names, and in some cases forge documentation, but that all adds to the challenge. Of course it helps when your husband has a state-of-the-art colour photocopier in his office.'

The guests again roared with laughter.

'Thank you, Mr Taxpayer,' said a beaming Stanton, proud of his skinny wife.

'Can anyone play this game?' asked Kinghorn enthusiastically.

'Definitely not,' replied Paloma, 'there's a very strict means test. You must earn over 100,000 dollars a year, drive a car worth over 60,000, and have at least half a million invested in the stock exchange.'

Horton Boner slapped his thigh in glee. This was some dinner party.

'It must be so exciting – even a little dangerous,' said Kinghorn, who'd never been near a foodbank in his life, except for a brief photo opportunity during the last election campaign.

'Wonderfully dangerous,' said Paloma. 'I nearly got caught out at the Presbyterian Social Services foodbank in Onehunga last month.'

Paloma detailed the story of her brush with the authorities to her enraptured audience: 'I helped them organise a corporate fund-raiser some years ago. One of the ladies helping at the foodbank recognised me from it. She swore she'd seen me before, but the fund-raiser was long enough ago that she couldn't quite place me. I had to think on my feet. The woman looked a tad dykey so I told her it may have been at a Women's Refuge a few years back after my husband raped and beat me.'

Again the guests hooted with laughter – especially Horton. He found the idea of raping his wife quite hilarious, given they hadn't slept together for a very long time. This was turning into a frightfully amusing evening.

'Did she buy your story?' asked a fascinated Gretchen van der Flanders.

'Hook, line and sinker,' confirmed Paloma. 'Stupid thing felt so sorry for me she offered a free women's self-defence course and stuffed an extra bag of oranges into the food parcel for the kids. It made a wonderful citrus sauce for the pheasant.'

Janet chimed in with a similar story. 'I tried the Poverty Action foodbank in Wellington. It's far easier than the Salvation Army. They're all do-gooding socialists so, as long as you blame that "fascist bastard" Norman Kinghorn and his government for your plight, they'll give you anything you want.'

'Fascist bastard?' said Kinghorn delightedly. 'Did you really say that?'

'Yes, and it worked a charm, you fascist bastard,' joked

Janet, as the Prime Minister roared with laughter. Norman really liked Janet Stanton, so much so that sometimes he found it difficult to keep his hands off her. Actually, when David Stanton was out of the room, he didn't keep his hands off her, and she never let out a word of complaint.

'The Sallies were far more difficult,' explained Janet. 'They wanted my name and proof that I was receiving a benefit to ensure I wasn't ripping them off. Since Norman's latest welfare cuts were approved, there's been such an upsurge in demand they've had to become much stricter.'

'I told you that Bill would lead to efficiencies,' said Kinghorn proudly. 'It's good to know the charities are stepping in and doing the job.'

'The only identification I had on me was my American Express Gold Card,' said Janet, to more uproarious laughter from all the guests, 'but I knew that wouldn't work. Fortunately, some months ago I found some poor solo mother's Community Services Card lying in the street and I'd forgotten to return it. I simply gave this woman's name and produced the card.'

'Well done, Janet,' replied Horton Boner, most impressed. 'That's what I call enterprise.'

'And it reminds me that we've got to bring in photo IDs for all beneficiaries,' announced Kinghorn sternly. 'For all we know, thousands of New Zealanders could be going to foodbanks and getting a free, undeserved meal just like Janet here. Thank you for bringing it to my attention.'

'The card certainly did the trick,' continued Janet. 'They handed over a bag of groceries and gave me an Unemployment is Not Working sticker. I didn't tell them it was a bit small for the SUV.'

Everyone hooted yet again. Stanton wished all the left-wing commentators out there could see that the New Right did have a sense of humour. The guests all agreed that they would try out Foodbanquet at their next dinner party. It was far more entertaining than hiring a string quartet, or even a stripogram.

'I still don't understand,' said David Stanton, 'how you could cook that entire meal with just one foodbank parcel.'

'Easy,' said his wife. 'The tripe or La Tripe Povertée as I call it, was just a kilo of tripe with a few onions.'

'What about the paua?' asked Horton Boner. 'You can't tell me they hand out some of the most expensive seafood in the country at a foodbank. That's taking welfarism too far.'

'You two don't quite understand the rules of the game,' explained Paloma smilingly. 'If you can get other food by swapping the contents of your foodbank parcel, then that's allowed – as long as you don't spend any money of your own.'

'Or use credit cards,' added Janet. 'You see, there were lots of Maoris at the foodbank.'

'Typical,' thundered Tipene angrily. 'Forget Ngapuhi – the biggest iwi in this country is Ngati Bloody Welfare.'

'Hear, hear,' added Gretchen, and smiled warmly at the man she had earlier insulted.

Janet continued her story. 'And two of the Maoris I met at the foodbank had just been skin diving. All I did was offer them a packet of Mallowpuffs from my food parcel if they would swap a couple of bags of baby paua.'

'That's an extremely good bargain,' commented Kinghorn.

'Mallowpuffs in a foodbank parcel?' spluttered Horton indignantly, almost choking on his shiraz. 'I can tolerate cabin bread, and perhaps a packet of wine biscuits on special occasions, but chocolate-covered Mallowpuffs in a food package meant for beneficiaries is taking this five star welfare state too far! We need to send a get-tough message to these welfare recipients. That will shake them out of their comfort zone while they're sitting at home watching their SKY TV.'

'Well, I did tell the Maoris that if they didn't agree to my little "tiriti",' chuckled Janet, 'I'd ring up Fisheries and dob them in for poaching.'

'Now I get it,' said Kinghorn, '*poached* baby paua on a bed of spinach.'

Everyone roared with laughter. More wine flowed, and everyone agreed that they could not remember a more enjoyable dinner party in their entire lives. So great was the fun had at the event that the stunning social success of Boner's fiftieth party just a few weeks ago faded into the background and became a distant memory.

'So every single item was either given to you for free or you bartered for it,' said David Stanton suspiciously as he passed around the port wine and cigars.

'Of course,' rejoined his wife.

'I would have sworn that the lamb's fry was marinated in something alcoholic – vermouth or brandy or something. I know those beneficiaries and what-have-you get a bloody easy ride, but as far as I'm aware, you *cannot* get alcohol at a foodbank.'

'Close but no cigar, my dear,' replied Janet, as she lit Horton Boner's very expensive Cohiba. 'It was marinated in meths.'

The other guests almost choked.

'Methylated spirits?' exclaimed a horrified Gretchen van der Flanders.

'Don't worry, you won't go blind,' said Janet calmly. 'I only used a splash for flavour. It's a great tenderiser and really high-lights the flavour of offal – especially if you're drinking a slightly fruity white wine. The gewürz was a good choice, David.'

Her husband grinned.

'Bought a case when we went up to Hawke's Bay to the opera in the vineyard,' he explained proudly.

'So what did you do? Swap a loaf of bread with some tramp at the foodbank to get the meths?' asked Horton, intrigued.

'No way,' explained Janet firmly, 'he was at the night shelter.'

'It did marinate the liver rather nicely,' remarked Norman Kinghorn. The guests heartily agreed, though Janet had to caution Kinghorn against using meths as a substitute in a martini if he ever ran out of vermouth.

'So what do you call the meths dish?' asked Paloma Boner.

'Lamb's Fry du Nuit,' explained the hostess. 'Everyone thinks the "nuit" refers to the dark colour of the liver, but of course it refers to the night shelter. I recently gave the recipe to a celebrity cookbook – without the meths of course. All funds raised save starving children in Somalia.'

'Good on ya,' added Horton Boner, 'but I hope we're not developing too much of a welfare mentality with those starving kiddies. We don't want to make them overly reliant on foreign aid.'

'Exactly,' agreed Tipene. 'Welfare dependency is far more dangerous than famine. Before giving I'd like to know just how many of those Somalis really are starving. I suspect a lot just don't want to go to work.'

'I heard of a group of fourteen Somalis that periodically went off for holidays in the Seychelles, staying at luxury resorts,' explained Horton Boner, 'yet they were pleading starvation and getting aid from Oxfam.'

'Exactly,' said Paloma Boner. 'Probably had a TV satellite dish on the thatched roof of their hut.'

'You're dead right,' agreed Gretchen. 'My friend's husband owns a company that installs cable television receivers around the world. Somalia's one of the biggest markets for new receivers, after the Sudan,' she explained.

'Ungrateful bastards,' hissed Paloma.

Norman Kinghorn sculled his beer, wiped his face with a serviette, which was actually a place mat but he hadn't noticed, and let out a very satisfied burp.

'Janet Stanton,' announced Prime Minister Kinghorn, 'that's by far the best meal I've had in ages.'

'Hear, hear,' agreed all the guests.

'It amazes me,' remarked Horton Boner, 'how people complain they can't live on the unemployment benefit when you can serve up a gourmet feast like that on one foodbank parcel. And you didn't even have to use vegetables from your garden.'

'Which is allowed under the rules of the game,' added Paloma.

'Hold on,' said David Stanton suspiciously, as he sniffed the aroma of the large plunger of fresh coffee that Janet had just placed on the table. 'You can't tell me that the foodbank are giving away the very best arabica coffee.'

'Of course not,' replied Janet calmly. 'That's why I had to steal it.'

There was a horrified silence.

'Don't worry,' reported a relaxed Paloma. 'Janet hasn't broken the rules of the game. One of the rules of Foodbanquet is that if you can't find the necessary ingredients in your foodbank parcel, you're allowed to trade or steal to get what you want. Many beneficiaries do it every day of their lives.'

'She's right,' said Tipene. 'Forget unemployment or child abuse, one of the biggest social problems facing our country is the loss of profits to big retail businesses because of shoplifting.'

'True,' agreed the Prime Minister, 'but I must say, Janet, to go out into a supermarket or whatever and steal a packet of superb arabica coffee is a very courageous and enterprising act.'

Janet Stanton blushed and smiled coquettishly at Kinghorn.

Her husband was not so impressed.

'Darling, I've just commissioned Gary Gunson to write a thirty-page speech denouncing shoplifting as a major abuse of human rights. The Prime Minister is delivering it to the National Association of Retail Greengrocers in less than a week. It would hardly look good if the wife of the Prime Minister's Chief Political Adviser was convicted of shoplifting.'

'But I didn't get caught,' giggled Janet, and everyone roared with laughter. 'That's what makes the game so much fun. It's totally risky!'

'That's not the point,' replied David Stanton angrily. 'You might have!'

'Lighten up, Stanton,' advised his boss calmly. 'Where's your sense of adventure, man? She didn't get caught, did she? She's far too clever to get caught.'

David Stanton reluctantly agreed, and after more wine and lots of intelligent, enjoyable conversation, it became time for the guests to leave.

'Bags the next round of Foodbanquet is at my house,' said Kinghorn.

'If you insist, Prime Minister,' replied Janet graciously, 'but won't it be difficult for you to disguise yourself in a foodbank?'

'Not as difficult as shoplifting some gourmet coffee,' laughed Kinghorn. 'Maybe I'll get your husband to steal the coffee for me. After all, he is my assistant.'

Again, the assembled guests roared, with the exception of Stanton.

'Anyway,' continued Kinghorn, 'I have a lovely make-up assistant who slaps on the talc every time I do a television interview. Having to disguise me so I could fool the staff of a foodbank will give her a challenge. I've always told the Opposition that a fulltime make-up artist would not be a waste of government funds.'

As Kinghorn rose to leave, the assembled guests also rose. The ladies kissed him warmly and the gentlemen shook his hand vigorously, and every single one of them agreed that it was wonderful to see that their blundering Prime Minister was finally developing a sense of humour.

# JENNIFER LANE

Jennifer Lane was born in 1972 on the south coast of New South Wales. In 1995 she crossed the world to see what life was like in a foreign hemisphere, only to meet a Kiwi and move with him to Wellington. Whether it was because she knew no one and had no job, or because she finally felt inspired, she penned her first short story within a month of settling in New Zealand. She has continued writing over the years, sneaking in an hour here, five minutes there, and has enjoyed some success with short stories. Now taking time out of the real world to care for her daughter, she's attempting to write 'the novel'. 'Scout's Honour' is an excerpt from this novel, entitled (this week, anyway) *Little White Lies*.

# SCOUT'S HONOUR

Mum was already five months' pregnant, her body puffed up like a pink marshmallow, when Dr Bryce declared that he could hear not one but two heartbeats.

'You what? You can hear my ticker from down there?' Mum asked. Her bloated face was streaked with sweat. While pregnancy is kind to some women, it was particularly cruel to Mum. Her face was swollen and blotchy, her blonde hair limp and greasy.

'Twins, Mrs Barrett. You are carrying twins,' Dr Bryce said, scratching a tuft of white hair that sprayed out of his ear like water from a hose.

'What? Two of them?' Mum attempted to sit up on the narrow bed she was lying on, but the full extent of Dr Bryce's words sunk in and she flopped back heavily. 'Jesus!'

My younger brother Elijah and me sat squashed together in the surgery's only spare chair. I remember being surprised, not that there were going to be two more Elijahs instead of just one, but that Dr Bryce could hear Mum through all the hair that sprouted from his ears.

Mum later told the twins that their conception was a peace-offering from Dad, that they were the result of a row that dragged on for two weeks. Although Mum and Dad disagreed more than they agreed, I'll never forget that fight. Elijah and I gave it a score of nine out of ten, with anything over six being Red Alert – our secret code for escaping to the safety of the secret room under the stairs. Despite the fact that we shared the secret room with the vacuum cleaner, mop, bucket, broom, smelly rags, bottles of bleach and cans of cleaning spray, it was our sanctuary. With the little white door closed behind us, Mum and Dad's voices sounded far away, as if all the arguing and rude words came from the Irwin's place, not ours. Over those two weeks we spent so much time behind the door that we carried the smell of cleaning products, of detergent and bleach, in our hair, skin and clothes. Some of the kids teased me about it at school. 'Bog girl,' hot peanut-butter-breath sang in my face, 'Evie stinks like a bog.' It didn't bother me. Mum called Dad much worse things. And at least I smelt like a clean bog.

The fight coincided, as many of them did, with one of Mrs Lothum's visits. Mrs Lothum dropped by every Friday – after she'd finished her shift at the Post Office and while Grandma Bett was cleaning the church. She said she chose to come on

Fridays because Mum needed the company, but a more likely story was she knew that Grandma Bett wouldn't stand for her gossip.

Mrs Lothum looked like she belonged on the Saturday morning cartoons, along with Bugs Bunny and Porky Pig. She was big in the middle with a tiny head and sticks for legs, as if she was made of plasticine and had been squeezed at both ends. Her head size was compensated for by an overly generous helping of hair which she regularly dyed different shades of brightest orange and red. She had been in Mum and Dad's year at Coongahoola High, and from what she later told me, almost certainly would have liked to marry Dad herself. 'Every girl in the school dreamt of becoming Mrs Barrett,' she had confided in me. 'Next to him, none of the other boys mattered.' Keeping tabs on Dad was bound to have been her main motive for being such good friends with Mum. She and Mum had never been friends at school, yet it was Mrs Lothum's hand Mum dug her nails into when I made my untimely entrance into the world. And it was Mrs Lothum Mum asked to be my godmother.

The afternoon of the fight, Elijah and I had dumped our school bags under the wobbly coat rack in the hallway and run into the kitchen to find Mrs Lothum and Mum seated on either side of a plate of Grandma Bett's Anzac biscuits. Mrs Lothum was whispering and making noises of disapproval; Mum was clenching her fists. By the time Mrs Lothum had eaten all but the last of the biscuits (a broken one), Mum's cheeks were scribbled with tears.

We'd started eating tea and Mum had looked at her watch fifteen times before Dad's grease-smeared face appeared in the kitchen. I used to say he looked like Harrison Ford from the Indiana Jones movies, but only because that's what Dad said himself. I thought he was better looking than Harrison Ford, even with his two rude tattoos.

Dad sat down next to Elijah, and Mum slapped a plate of burnt sausages and vegetable mush in front of him. Peas slid off the side of his plate, bounced onto the table and rolled plop, plop, plop onto the worn brown lino floor. I wished I'd had a chance to warn him.

'So tell me again why you've been doing so much overtime this last week?' Mum demanded, her still-clenched fists digging into her narrow hips.

'I told you before,' Dad replied, with a mouthful of watery cabbage. 'There's a lot of blokes away this time of year. Fishin' an' stuff. Boatin', goin' bush.' He wiped his chin with the back of his hand.

'A lot of blokes away? I see. So that's why Nurse Audrey has to settle for some bastard who's married.'

Mum was shaking, her breathing was shallow and quick, and her jaw was clenched. I wanted more than anything to hear Grandma Bett's keys rattle in the front door, but knew that was unlikely. The whole of Coongahoola had gone crazy that week. Word had got out that Martha Mills saw a vision of the Virgin Mary near the Bagooli River, and the religious sect, the Believers, began moving to town. It was the biggest thing to ever happen to Coongahoola, and being an active member of the Catholic church, Grandma Bett had back-to-back meetings to attend.

'What're you gettin' at, Nell?' Dad asked, sawing through his sausage. His feet were shifting under the table. He kept his eyes on his plate.

'What do you think I'm getting at? Have you been paying Nurse Audrey visits? Visits of a non-medical kind?' These were the words we'd heard Mrs Lothum whisper. I wondered again what a 'non-medical kind' of visit was.

'Nurse Audrey?' Dad pretended to laugh, but I think he really wanted to cry. He looked at Elijah and me, but both of us knew better than to say anything. 'Oh, you know old Aud,' he said finally, spearing the half sausage on his plate.

'Yeah I do, matter of fact. She was at both the kids' births, which is more than I can say for you.'

'You know how bossy she is, then. Tried saying no to her? Bet you just did what you were told.'

'And what's that s'posed to mean?'

Dad dropped his knife and fork and shrugged. 'What choice did I have eh, Nell? Come on, it meant nothing. The woman's built like a brick shithouse. Ugly as sin.'

With that, Mum threw a handful of peas at Dad (they'd been in her fist all along, waiting for the cue), beginning two weeks of yelling, plate-smashing, door-slamming and furniture-kicking, of slapped-together school lunches, sloppier than usual dinners and tight-lipped goodnight kisses. Dad reacted in his usual way: sitting on the front steps rolling tiny cigarettes, or wandering the house with his hands stuffed in his pockets, pouting and keeping his Jersey cow eyes downcast, a tactic Elijah (who'd inherited Dad's eyes) adopted whenever he was in trouble (his teachers fell for it, just as Mum eventually did).

At least five of Grandma Bett's good china dinner plates and three ceramic duck ornaments had been shattered before Dad's eyes finally melted Mum's anger. Mum had just hurled one of their few remaining wedding photos at the kitchen wall, cutting through the green and orange swirls on Grandma Bett's wallpaper and spraying glass across the lino. She looked at Dad through teary eyes and dropped onto her knees. Then she begged him to promise he wouldn't do it again.

Dad leant against the fridge, slowly moved his eyes from the shards of glass to Mum's pleading eyes, and lifted the fingers on his left hand in a Scout's Honour salute. While Dad was never a member of Scouts, his workmate Derek had been, and Derek always offered the Scout's Honour salute in the place of a promise. (The reason being, he'd explained to Dad and Dad later explained to Elijah (and Elijah to me), that the Scout's Honour wasn't like a real promise. It was just something a Scoutmaster, more than likely an American, maybe even one of those sicko paedophile Scoutmasters, came up with. And as he was no longer a Scout – and Dad had never been one – it didn't bind them to anything.)

Mum didn't know that Dad was never a Scout, nor did she care. She was so relieved by his response that she must've forgotten that she was no longer a schoolgirl. She must've forgotten that she was now a mother of two and that the two were eating fish fingers and mashed potato at the kitchen table, just a few feet away from where she knelt in her baggy grey tracksuit pants because she then asked Dad to love her like he did that first night in his Ford station wagon. Dad answered her not by speaking, but by wrapping his tattooed arms around her, lifting her up and carrying her into the hallway on his shoulder. Grandma Bett suddenly appeared (like us, she often disappeared when Mum and Dad were fighting. Elijah and I wondered whether she had a Red Alert of her own) and shooed us, still chewing our fish fingers and clutching our plates, downstairs into the laundry, coughing loudly even though she didn't have a cold.

'After two weeks of nothing, and with all that anger finally let go, it was twice as good as usual,' Mum later told the twins, who nodded as if they had an inkling of what she was talking about. 'Should've been no surprise there were two of you.'

Always doing things in pairs, the twins had arrived not one but two months before the date Grandma Bett had circled on the Coongahoola Steelworks calendar that hung on the side of the fridge. That night Elijah and me were plucked from our sleep and plonked into our car seats. All I remember of the midnight adventure was Mrs Lothum opening her front door. It was as if I was still dreaming. She was wearing a pink floral nightie so thin you could see her lacy underwear through it, and though she said she'd just got out of bed, her lips were painted hot pink and her bright red hair was piled up neatly on her head, like a soft-serve ice cream. She looked more like a cartoon character than ever. We stood, blinking sleep out of our eyes, on either side of Dad, wearing our pyjamas and holding the plastic bags Grandma Bett had stuffed with our clothes.

On the way to the hospital the next morning, Mrs Lothum asked us so many questions about Dad that Elijah asked, 'Do you want to marry our daddy?' She didn't speak to us for the rest of the journey and drove so fast that I slid off the back seat when the car skidded into the car park. She squeezed our hands, a little more tightly than necessary I thought, as she dragged us down the shiny orange corridor and shoved us into the maternity ward.

There were six beds in the ward; three of them held sleeping women. Two of the sleeping women's faces were obscured by long blue veils; the other was Mum's. Her mouth was half-opened, as if she'd been about to say something but had fallen asleep before she'd got the words out, and one arm flopped off the edge of the bed.

Grandma Bett sat on the other side of Mum's bed, knitting needles in hand and a large ball of red wool on her lap.

'Ready to meet your baby brother and sister?' she whispered.

Leading us out of the ward, Grandma Bett glanced over at the sleeping, veiled women and the large wooden crosses that hung over each of their beds. She shook her head, crossed herself and moved her lips in prayer.

We were shuffled over to the crib on the farthest side of the neonatal unit. Inside it, lying side by side, were two tiny pink creatures. Two tiny pink creatures who were soon to sleep in our room, play with our toys, and share the tub of vanilla and chocolate chip ice cream Mum brought home from Woolworths each week.

'Evie, Eli, say hello to dear little Gabriel Alexander and Lucy Grace,' Grandma Bett said.

'Hello Gabriel Alexander and Lucy Grace,' Elijah and I chorused, in the same monotone tune we usually reserved for greeting our teachers each morning, and although we were old enough to know not to expect a reply, we were disappointed by the reception we were given. Lucy shrieked and turned her face away from us.

I stood on my tippy-toes and peered down at the twins, who would later become known as Grub and Lucky. Their eyes were squeezed shut, as if they were wishing they were somewhere else, and they were so small they reminded me of guinea pigs. Gabriel's head was shaped like an upside down ice cream cone, and even though Lucy was supposed to be a girl, she had less fuzz on her head than Gabriel. They didn't look like the babies I'd seen on TV.

'Are you sure they're ours?' Elijah asked. 'Aren't they a bit small?'

'Give them time, Eli,' Grandma Bett replied, 'they'll soon grow into themselves. You'll see.'

It took four weeks for the twins to fit into their wrinkly pink skins and turn into proper babies, and until then the hospital was our after-school playground. We watched as women in veils came and went. Their only visitors were other women and girls, never their husbands or sons. Grandma Bett told us that the Believers regarded childbirth as women's business, that the men only received their children once they were brought to the camp, little clean pink bundles swaddled in white; all the messy stuff, the blood and gunk, having been taken care of. 'What kind of nonsense is that?' Grandma Bett muttered.

Dad visited when he could, usually on weekends, and only under Mum and Grandma Bett's close supervision. This was because of Nurse Audrey. Back then I didn't know what she and Dad had done, but I knew it was bad and I was scared of her. She was bigger than Dad and bossier than Grandma Bett. The long black hair she scraped up into a bun every morning spilt out during the day, giving it the appearance of an overgrown garden, and whenever she squeezed past us we'd feel, pressing against us, the softness of what Elijah would call her 'bazoobas'. Whatever she and Dad had done, I knew she'd made him do it.

But Nurse Audrey was impossible to avoid, since she was the one who cared for the twins. The twins that, unbeknownst to her, she had helped create. I watched her closely and saw that she was even gentler with them than she was with the other babies in the neonatal unit, standing and watching over them like Grandma Bett always did. She whispered things to them too, something about their daddy, though I never heard what.

What I remember most about Lucy and Gabriel as babies is the sound of Lucy's voice. It was as if there was some kind of mix-up in Mum's tummy and Lucy ended up with Gabriel's cry as well as her own; Lucy screeched for two while Gabriel hardly made a peep. Apart from the eternal howl coming from Lucy's end of the cot, nothing particularly memorable happened until the twins reached the age of two. My recollection of them then – Lucy's angry, red-raw face, Gabriel's Vegemite smile – is very clear. It was about this age that they became known as Lucky and Grub.

Lucy became Lucky because that was how Grub pronounced her name. It seemed fitting enough to Elijah and me. Lucy cried so much that we were convinced she was going to die, so every morning her tiny, watery eyes opened we felt she was lucky.

Gabriel was called Grub for more obvious reasons. Unlike all the other toddlers we knew, he didn't move on from the baby phase of tasting everything he could get his little fingers on. He was still supplementing his diet of Weetbix, toast, mashed vegetables and Grandma Bett's shepherd's pies with insects, dirt, leaves and whatever he could lick out from between the floorboards by the time he turned two, and by then he was so covered in grot it didn't matter what he did, he was permanently dirty. Even after Grandma Bett stopped spreading Vegemite on his toast, somehow his face and hands were always smeared with it.

Grub's predisposition to filth wasn't helped by the fact that he was given more freedom than any of us. Back then they didn't know why Lucky was born so angry (she was later diagnosed with an ear problem), but Grandma Bett embraced the challenge of nursing her to happiness. That left Mum in charge of Grub. I've looked back at some photos of that time and wondered whether Mum was taking care of herself, let alone Grub. It looked as though her wardrobe had merged with Dad's, her clothes were so baggy and shabby. And it could've just been Dad's poor photography skills, but her face looked almost yellow, the same colour as her greasy, unkempt hair.

But the big thing that happened during the twins' second year, and the reason why I remember it so vividly, was a result of Grub sticking my strawberry rubber up his nose. My best friend Shelly Sanderson had given me the rubber for Christmas – they were the craze then – and it never occurred to me to hide it from Grub like we did our crayons, paint and plasticine. If I had any idea of what trouble it would bring, I would've chucked it in the bin, especially since it made more mess than it erased, turning minor spelling mistakes into ugly black smudges. It was the size and shape of a strawberry and had a sickly strawberry, rubbery scent. Even now when I think of strawberries I feel queasy.

It happened during the last week of the Christmas school holidays. Elijah and I were in the secret room working on our new wallpaper, having grown bored of the dinosaurs we'd sticky-taped over the walls after school broke up. Lucky's screaming at nothing and Mum's yelling at Dad meant that Elijah and I spent more and more time in the secret room. We'd go straight there after we'd finished playing outside and we'd stay until the lure of TV grew too strong or Mum summoned us for tea.

'Aaaaaahhhhhhhh!' The secret room muffled some of the noise, but this groan was loud enough for both of us to drop our paintbrushes.

'Yaaaaaahhh!' We heard it again and this time Elijah's eyes widened in horror.

'Grub!' he cried and scrambled out of the little door. I followed him, nearly tripping over my sneakers.

We weren't used to hearing Grub's voice. This sound was more harrowing than any in Lucky's repertoire and we knew she wasn't home. Grandma Bett had taken her to church for her daily blessing.

We found Grub sitting cross-legged on Charlemagne's rug (so called for the kitten Elijah had run over on it with his tricycle), tears streaking his dirt-stained cheeks, grubby hands clasped over his nose.

'What's wrong? Grub?' I knelt down beside him and wiped a sticky cheek with my finger. He smelt like wet soil.

Grub was a blond version of Elijah, though instead of brown, his big cow eyes were a deep sea-blue (I could easily imagine Mrs Lothum saying that the males got all the looks in our family). His long black lashes were plastered together with tears, reminding me of my paintbrush. He lifted his hands and revealed a nose that had ballooned to almost double its size. I gasped, thinking it was about to explode.

'Stuff's coming out his nose!' Elijah cried.

I leant in closer and saw a little green stalk poking out of his left nostril. 'Jeepers, that's my strawberry!'

Grub started rocking, blubbering.

'Muuuuum!' Elijah yelled. 'Muuuuum! Grub's got Evie's rubber up his nose. Muuuuuuum!'

Mum scuffed into the living room in her pink fluffy-bunny slippers. Her eyes were red and puffy. Dad'd got home after us kids'd gone to bed the night before and she'd been waiting for him, clomping up and down the hall, calling him the kind of names we'd get detention for saying at school.

Something got smashed when the front door finally clicked open, something brown and shiny. Another ceramic duck maybe. Elijah couldn't find all the pieces of it this morning to work out exactly what it was.

'Grub's got what up where?' Mum asked, pulling her dressing gown around herself and tying up its cord. She lifted Grub up and studied his swollen nose. 'Oh poor baby. Evie, try and get it out, pet.'

'Me?' Mum had no idea how big my strawberry was in relation to Grub's nostril.

'You've got a steady hand, love. I've seen those pictures you paint. Give it a go. I'll hold him.' Mum knelt down and propped Grub up on her lap. His face was ghostly white.

'Noooooo!' Grub cried, and I saw that Mum had tears in her eyes.

'Shhhh, bub, it'll be OK.' Mum held Grub's hands away from his face. 'Go on, Evie!'

The plastic stalk was slippery and warm. I took it between my thumb and index finger and gently pulled. It was like activating Grub's 'on' switch. The more I tugged, the louder he screeched.

'I can't do it – his nose is going to rip.'

'Can I've a go?' Elijah asked.

'No!' Mum snapped, then she chewed on her little finger, something she did when she didn't know what to do next.

'Get your shoes, you two,' she said finally, 'we'll take him to Dr Bryce.'

Dad had given Derek a lift to work that day, so we had to catch the bus. I was relieved that no one from school was on it. Mum covered Grub's face with a tea towel so people wouldn't look at us, but they stared anyway. I even caught two of the Believers watching as we walked down the aisle. I couldn't understand what fascinated them – apart from the kangaroos on Grub's tea towel, there was little difference between it and the blue veils they wore on their heads. Luckily, Mr Buckley and Noodle were also on the bus and Noodle lifted his leg and weed on Mrs Valentine's bag of groceries. Everyone was too busy trying not to laugh to bother asking us why Grub had a tea towel on his head.

Mum made Elijah and me play in the waiting room while she and Grub were in with Dr Bryce. I hated the waiting room – it stunk of sick people and their horrible medicines. Elijah started running down the corridor to the toilet door and back again – he wanted to see how many times he could do it before Dr Bryce fixed Grub's nose. I sat on one of the green chairs that farted every time you sat down and flipped through what was left of a *Woman's Weekly* after people had ripped out the pages that were worth reading. There was a toy box next to the fish tank in the corner but its only contents were a plastic pull-along caterpillar, a polar bear with chewed ears and a wooden tiger puzzle that was missing half its pieces. Jonathan Frawley from my class was also in the waiting room. He mustn't have wanted me to know he was with his mum because he moved a seat away from her and picked up a falling-apart magazine about motorbikes. Silly thing was, she had the same freckly face and red hair as him, so I knew straight away who she was. She wore a purple and white striped shirt and had put her make-up on neatly. I remember thinking that I'd have been proud to be seen with his mum.

When Grub wobbled out of Dr Bryce's room on his stumpy little legs, I was relieved to see that he still had a nose, even if it was as big and swollen as a clown's. He was clutching the strawberry Dr Bryce had prised out with a long pair of tweezers, and when he saw Elijah and me, he proudly waved it at us, smiling. I wondered whether it still smelt of strawberries or if his nose'd sniffed up all its scent.

It was usually windy in Coongahoola – I was used to looking at the world from behind the strands of hair that always blew in my face – but that day was strangely still. The bus pulled up at 2:02 p.m., the exact time it was due, which was also unusual. Elijah had sprinted up the road so Mum had to yell at him to get back, quick smart. I wouldn't say I was psychic, but I did have an uncomfortable feeling when I climbed onto the bus. I was looking out at the towering gum trees – at their silver leaves, silent and still – when I saw our station wagon. The bus was winding around Emerson Street and our once-white Ford station wagon was parked in front of a cream brick house. You couldn't miss it. It was older than any of us kids and had a dent in the back from where Mum backed over Dad's motorbike (a long story which Mum paid me five dollars to keep to myself). Its rusting number plate read XLB098. 'Stands for Extra Large Boy,' Dad had once said, winking at Elijah.

'Hey! Look!' Elijah had noticed the car too. 'What's Dad doing . . .' just as he spoke, Elijah realised he shouldn't have, '. . . here.' He finished with a whisper and slowly turned around to look at Mum.

'Next stop, Andy,' Mum called out to Mr McEwan, the bus driver. Her teeth were clenched and her reddening face glistened with sweat.

The other people on the bus had seen our station wagon too. They knew something was going on – you could tell by the way they kept sneaking glances at Mum. Just as well

Mrs Lothum wasn't on the bus – the whole world would've known by tea time.

'You two go straight home,' Mum said without looking at us and she walked up the aisle carrying Grub under one arm.

Elijah and I raced to the back of the bus, kneeled on the sticky vinyl back seat and watched out the window as Mum stormed up the footpath towards the cream house. I wished for her sake she'd worn something nice, like the red dress Grandma Bett had helped Dad buy her for Christmas. She was wearing Dad's grey Coongahoola Steelworks T-shirt and faded old jeans, which hung off her as if she was a coat hanger. She hadn't bothered to do anything with her straw-like hair, not even comb it. I wanted her to look nicer than all the other mothers in Coongahoola so Dad would like only her. Grub didn't look out of place under her wet armpit. He only had one sock on, and it must've belonged to Lucky because it was bright pink. One hand was touching his bruised nose and the other was still holding onto the strawberry rubber as if it were something very precious.

Mum slammed the front door and stormed down the hallway about an hour after we'd got home. I made Elijah go out and check how angry her face was.

'Like Lucky's,' he reported, closing the secret door behind him. 'All snotty.'

Dad didn't come home at all that night. Or the next. We discovered that the cream house belonged to Frannie Larson from Frannie's Fashion for Larger Ladies. Mum was yelling about her at Derek over the back fence.

'So you're telling me you had no idea he was dropping you off and running off to Fat Frannie's?' she demanded in a voice that half of our street could hear. Our ears couldn't pick up what Derek said back, but Mum yelled, 'Scout's Honour, my arse!' and stomped back up the back steps.

We knew Dad did some wrong things because he was always in trouble with Mum and Grandma Bett, but he sometimes gave us fifty cents, which was double the amount Mum ever gave us, and he was never cranky with us. I missed hearing the floorboards creaking under his boots. I wouldn't have minded listening to Mum yelling and breaking things if only I could've heard the sound of Dad's boots.

'Maybe Mum killed him,' Elijah suggested after a week of no Dad. I tried to picture Dad lying squashed like poor Charlemagne on a rug in Frannie Larson's house, but I couldn't. Unless she had a really big rug. Then a couple of days later, Elijah overheard Grandma Bett on the phone. 'Wait it out, son,' she whispered. Son! It could only have been Dad. We were so relieved we painted smiley pictures of him and plastered them all over the secret room. We didn't know if we'd ever see him again, but at least we knew he was alive.

# TRACEY SLAUGHTER

Tracey Slaughter's first collection of poems and short stories, *Her Body Rises*, was published by Random House in 2005. She has won the Bank of New Zealand Katherine Mansfield Novice Writer's Award, the Bank of New Zealand Katherine Mansfield Premier Writer's Award, the Aoraki Festival Poetry Competition and been highly commended in the *Sunday Star-Times* Short Story Competition. Her work has appeared in literary journals in New Zealand, the United Kingdom and France and in local anthologies. Slaughter studied at the University of Auckland and went on to teach there and at Massey University. She now writes fulltime and lives in Thames with her partner and two young children.

# NOTE LEFT ON A WINDOW

I had sex with the hitchhiker down on the beach, because I couldn't bear to take him into the caravan. By that stage I knew he wasn't the dangerous type, but I also knew a part of me had hoped that he was. He was just dirty in that arty way; I'd pulled up expecting something criminal, but I'd got a thinker, equally unclean but without the cruel streak. I should have guessed from the image of Che Guevara on his op-shop shirt, the sideways visionary stare unclouded by the grease. I might have wanted to take someone derelict, someone mean, to the caravan, a guy who'd fill its room with smoke and the mechanical racket of a sudden hard fuck, someone prone to smashing up things that deserved it the way that caravan did. But I couldn't have stood gentleness there, or thought. What I had wanted was a kind of assault: what I got was method, tenderness. It was bad enough down on the beach, his stroking approach to the places I wanted cracked open, his fingers exploratory, creeping slowly in and out of me as if following some kind of protocol. I could hardly stand such an analytical fuck: under his ribs and hips, the sadness almost rolled up from me, almost got loose from my eyelids. He murmured to me, proposals of touch, of entry; with knuckles and heels I clawed up and rammed him in. His hair fell forward and picked up sand and weed in pods and husks and star-shapes. I stared at that, and that was my mistake. His eyes were a forgery of Michael's, and so, I admit, for a while I clutched his face and the collarbone that spanned out into the angle of shadow that Michael's also sharpened to. The hitchhiker may as well have been Michael's twin.

The one good thing was his philosophy had the same effect as violence: he was too absorbed to pause and ask about a condom.

When I got inside the caravan later, I remembered a movie where a suicide note was left on a window. Someone breathed over all the glass in the dead one's room and there it was, a reason, a clue. Perhaps I had even watched that movie with Michael's warm head dumped, dozing, on my legs, the shaved hardness of his skull bedded back on my stomach. But I couldn't be sure that I had. And that thought – that I could not be certain of the place of his head, its dark mongrel cut, the dust that turned yellow and resinous along the curves of his ear, which I'd clean with my fingernail, poking him, teasing, *Scruffy bugger, for a spunky bastard you're a right grot* – the thought that I couldn't remember exactly where his body was when I watched that film, made me push round the caravan even more quickly, huffing on its windows until the whole metal hut sung and shivered on its chocks and I stood, clinging in the aisle in the middle, waiting for my ribs to remember the right way to breathe. I held on to the hooks on the row of skinny cupboards along the cabin and I thought of how he would've been too tall to stand up in here, thought of the black stubble over his skull pushed up against this squeaky ceiling, and slid my hands across it as if some grit might have stuck along there like Braille. And I thought of the thumb-sized dent behind his ear where I'd once discovered he'd picked up headlice from his little brother, and thrown his head off me like a ball, and then, calmer, yanked it back and scrubbed it till it foamed, then traced all his hair (it was long then) for the dead, gluey stars. I thought of the exact feeling of that, the delousing, his wet hair slipping up my fingerprints, the tiny hulls filtered down the length with my nails. It took so long to strain all of the eggs out that way, but I loved his hair, its wild black rigging. And then he cut it, probably tired of my scratching. I thought of the pulse in his neck I could look down over, then, lazy, half asleep myself, watching it flex in the haze from the fizzing television. But nothing I could remember was on the screen. Except the reflection of him.

Nothing was on the windows of the caravan, either. Webs, of course, a whole city of strings, triangular nests at the corners, sticky and dense, a complexity of clear lines trickling out. That was the film I watched while I stayed in the caravan the old lady had rented to me. It became so quiet I could hear the white scabs of fly bodies tapping on the windows. But I never saw a spider the whole time I was there.

The old lady's hair was the counterpart of the spiderwebs,

just as the asterisks of grass that blew on their parched rays around the caravan were the counterpart of the stars that had long, blurred spokes above it each night. Dusty wheels of grass; the stars that glared as hard as staples; the blues overlapping in Michael's iris like the stretched rings on his tie-dyed shirt: that's all my head let occur and recur as I spent my first days toking up in the caravan. I drank a bit too, but not a lot. Mostly I crouched on the steps, and the day patched into night, and I thought of the hub of diesel at the centre of Michael's eyes, the strokes of black that leached from it, warping the blueness. I smoked and looked outwards with my back to the room and sometimes it felt like Michael was in there behind me, his warm, untidy body taking up the whole coop: *Gizza durry*, he would have mumbled, sticking out a toe to nudge my neck, and the splints at the corners of the wagon would have creaked with his clumsiness. *Fuck off and get your own*, I would have said, then maybe gone to kiss him, nuzzling his thick lower lip that felt like flax. I wouldn't have gone out, staggering over the grass and hurling onto the sand dunes; the kind of sick that flies out like a liquid scream. Or even if I had, Michael would have held back my hair and whispered to me as I jerked: I would have known that I was not stifled, I was not extinct, because I could hear those whispers. Michael would have dug me up out of the sand and held me there kneeling, would have laughed and said, *I'm about to break the last commandment: never kiss a girl that's just puked.* Or maybe we would have brought his little brother with us, and we would try to stay mostly sober so somewhere in the night we could peel Smudge out of his sleeping bag and cart him to the long drop so he didn't piss his bunk, or even if we missed it, we wouldn't have made him feel like a criminal, belted him for it. So when I woke up the caravan might have smelt like pyjamas gone fuzzy with piss, and we might have spent the semi-dawn groaning at his brother to stop scuffling round and singing those chewed-up little TV tunes. *Dinosaurs, of all fucking predatory things, singing about happy families.* But even groggy, sleepless, it would have been good: it could've been, if we had ever come.

Instead I turned over somewhere about the fourth day and felt my brain in my head like a bruised fist, my guts like a dark alley leading to a messed-up face. The caravan was not a little family cocoon. It was a crypt. And at the door stood the old woman who had rented it to me. Obviously disgusted.

The old woman's hair was spiderweb, watered and combed across a tiny skull. It was scraped into a bun no thicker than one of her knuckles and stabbed in place with a wheel of yellow pins. I had seen her, over the last few days, when I surfaced, banging stakes into her garden with the back of a tomahawk, climbing up a ladder to a tilted birdhouse, scraping at the pelt of a mangy cat she held pinned to the lawn with a small implacable hand. She was miniature and ruthless. Mostly she'd ignored me, not out of hostility, but industry: she was simply too busy to be bothered with a waster like me. But at the door of the caravan she fixed me with eyes whose colours seemed to have dissolved beneath the lens, almost as clear as blisters except for the pinprick at the centre. That black fleck of pupil was shrewd.

After she stared at me she looked out over the lawn beyond the caravan. 'About time for drying out, I should think.'

Of course, she could have been talking about the lengths of rain above the section, so thin they were almost invisible and seemed to rise rather than drop. Even on the tin this rain was soundless, except for a sudden thicker slap. You could see a few of these darker patches twitching over the washing line, a weak sun exposed through them.

'I don't care,' I said, looking out. Even that light made my eyeballs ferment. When I talked I felt fibres break, crackle. My throat felt like tape.

'You'll come to,' the old woman said. 'If it lasts. If it sets in you'll be crying out for a change.'

In her grip was a plastic plate with one of the paper doilies you never see now. Dinky sausage rolls, biscuits cut into stars, a lamington bleeding grease and syrup. Just looking at it I could taste crystals, coconut the shape of the skin you chew away from your nails. Pastry, clumped and humid, forming a dam of butter behind your front teeth. She passed it to me, the gladwrap blurred with icing sugar.

'From down at my cardiac club. I told them I would fetch some leftovers back here for you. I always say you may as well take what you need. While it's offered you. Waste not, want not.'

She trudged away across the lawn in her rubber ankle boots. Her dress was checked with a tea towel pattern. Veins slithered through the tough skin of her calves. Before she turned at the brick verge of her house, she looked back once at me, a shaky rotation of her head. At that distance the discs of her eyes looked like liquid. I flattened myself against the door of the caravan. She would be kind but not lenient. Wondering what she guessed made me start to breathe badly.

It came to me, with a strange kind of longing, that there had been no one like her at Michael's funeral. There was no one catering, sorting, bustling, dishing round teas as if holding the cup straight was the first step in getting over a hard knock. As if survival was a process plodded towards through the small, ordinary routines. If the old woman had been at Michael's funeral I could imagine her closing her ragged lids, her blue-brown head with its wrinkle of bun nodding slowly in recognition. Then putting on her apron with a grim flick, directing me, away from despair, around the kitchen. But there was no one old. No one bleakly cheery. No one to pat you with a hand crooked with know-how, to tell you, *Chin up, you got to keep on.*

I wondered if that was why Michael had chosen her.

There were two kinds of people at Michael's funeral. And there was me, who belonged to neither of them.

Mostly I stayed with the university group, the circle Michael and I had met in the few months we'd spent together on campus. They loitered, in the consciously deranged clothes they paid too much for in chic charity shops. Over their tight, ancient dresses the women wore men's jackets still dense with working-class smells, smoko, Brylcreem, betting stubs. The male heads either spilled coils of ratted hair, or shone gauntly through caps of stubble; their glasses were two revolutionary circles, earnest and clear. They discussed Michael's death with me, monotone voices assembling the facts, intellectualising them. Some of the women touched my arm, blinked heavily, clasped the bone carvings at their necks. It was not that they did not care. But their mode of caring took place in their heads, in the effort to comprehend Michael's actions. Outside the church, a kind of impromptu tutorial was held, and Michael was material, a case study. I could see that here, as much as in their lectures, they were proud of their faculty for analysis, for stringent debate. I stood amongst their talk – Michael's *rationale*, his *choices* – and knew I would not be returning to any of my classes.

I'd thought Michael would last at university. It seemed

he had found his element. I'd watched him as he crouched in the quad, his elongated limbs curled around his satchel, squatting on the platforms to listen to a speaker, then straining forward in contention, illogical but charged. He had never had a chance like this in his life. His childhood had been too messy to achieve in; as an 'adult' student he closed everything out but ideas. All at once he read everything, stacks of scuffed Penguin Classics kicking round, shucked pages high-lighted and flapping from the fridge by magnets or pegged along the walls. But he read everything too late. The whole flat smelled like extinct theories, a nest of broken social contracts, disused principles. I took them all down after he died and dropped them in one swoop from the roof of the apartment block.

Outside the church on the day of his funeral, one of the university women started to talk of her own attempt. She had been meticulous, she said, from her first experiments, slicing vertically just below her elbow; she had mapped and planned, made annotations, she had compiled a kind of dissertation on death. It had defined her, the deadline she had set for finally extinguishing herself. She had worked towards it as she did for an assignment's due date. There was an academic chill in her voice, as if she still believed a razor could be pulled across a wrist in a postmodern sense.

I thought of how, when I dropped Michael's pages, they rippled into factions, all the great thinkers, hung or plunged through the shadows, hissed across the concrete forms, disappeared into the city.

The only other people at the funeral were the men who had been, or still were, in the life of Michael's mother.

Michael's mother was a slut and a slave.

By the end of the day of his funeral I had told her that to her face.

Perhaps it helped me to stand up through that day, it reinforced me, that hate. When she got up to read out a poem she had written for him, a current arced out from my spine, so strong I thought it might shatter some ribs. It was the rhyme, the da–di–da beat of what she was saying, the chattering, fuzzy effect. It was the fact that she really believed in the healing cuteness of what she had written, thought she could simper through some cheap scribble and that would help Michael, help all of us, *rest*. She rhymed that with *best*. Her head bobbed sweetly on the final rhymes. Once, her fingers even tapped on the altar rail, di–dum. She sucked in a lot of air as if her jingling voice was hindered by real grief. When she'd finished she staggered off delicately. I heard her graze her skinny arse past some man in the front row, notches of lace tugging open as she bent to coo her apology.

For the rest of the service I sat behind her and stared at her head, so tiny, so flat in its hood of hard gel. I stared at the two nodes of ear where her long clips dangled, the gutter of skin up the back of them, a white seam through the bottled glitter of her tan. I thought about how Michael had not liked his head once he'd shaved it, because it reminded him of his mother. I thought about being left with him for a while in the funeral home, climbing up to lever his head onto my lap, the vacant heavy orb of it, bristled and chill. I thought about the inquiring look on his face, the texture of his lower lip, mottled and dry, the scope of incoherent, soulful light that kept gathering and breaking on the lens of his eyes, although no soul was under them. It was just the wavelengths of emptied fibre shimmering at me. Catching and deflecting all that useless radiance.

I thought about how, very soon, that shimmer was going to be replaced. By the shimmer of his ash. By his ashes as they lifted, released, dispersed into shade, as they spread across everything, just for an instant, coated trees, stones, water, clung in currents of air like the form of a ghost. Then I would close and open my eyes, and all that dust would be breathed away, invisible. The outline of everything I saw would look sharp, detailed again, but empty. Haloed by his nothingness.

Right then, I knew that I could not leave him to his mother: she'd put the urn up somewhere gaudy, show it off for a few pissed days, she'd stroke it with her tacky hands, I could just hear her false nails clicking on it, the remains of her baby prickling at her touch. She'd stumble round the after party with it, yelling stories, rocking it down by her pelvic bone. She'd give up the act when the drinks hit double figures or something stronger rushed her brains. If she didn't spill him, Michael would end up on the bench somewhere among all the empty vessels. So I planned it, right then, how I would take him myself, although I didn't know yet that I'd drive him straight back to the caravan.

She had done a surgical job on her make-up, his mother. I noticed that when I went over to her after the funeral. Strokes of pencil were oily in the sparse fluff of her brows. Her lids were lined with black wedges, and the sockets shone with blues. She thought she could talk to me, that I would stand and listen to her melodic blabbing, the cadence of a born slag. While she prattled I could see in her body that she was aware of several men looking on. Her hips, working under the lace, her gaze, in its visor of sticky lashes, her talk, with its travesty of Michael-centred stories – highlights of his childhood that I knew were shit – everything about her was gauging the notice of men, as it always was. She was no more interested in me than she'd ever been in Michael. She would look you in the eye, but you could feel the pull of her attention, sleazy and lateral.

I told her what I thought of her. Michael wouldn't have liked me to be so cruel. He loved her the way a child loves a rodent or a bird, some mauled thing that you retrieve from a pulpy nest to watch it die slowly in a shoebox. But I had outgrown the idea of rescue. I knew hers came at the cost of her kids. When she was nourished she fluttered away to bring the next predator into their life. How she tracked them I just don't know: she had radar. When she was smacked-up once again she crawled into the corner of the kids' room and expected to be pitied, although by the stage her beatings were dished out the boys had already lived through weeks of their own. I thought she should have been put out of her misery long ago.

The funeral director must have sized her up anyway. It didn't take too much convincing to get him to hand over Michael to me instead. I paid: Michael's mother had told the guy she'd need welfare assistance to cover it. He had a mass of forms filled out in glitter pen, her printing loopy and babyish with oooo's and aaaaa's. But I put it down in cash, everything we had saved. Sometimes when Michael and I got somewhere in our savings we'd talked of a kind of future, of things we could use the money to try to set right: mostly we'd talk of taking Smudge from his mother, of trying to keep him safe. We had thought it probably wouldn't be hard to make her cave in and leave him for good; she wasn't much interested, except in the welfare, and sometimes we had Smudge camped out for weeks, while she was AWOL, toasted or 'in love'.

When I tipped the money onto the desk at the funeral

home I thought about that. I thought maybe I should be using it to take home the living son, not the dead one.

It might have been the thought of that that made me so angry when I got Michael's canister that I kicked it under the back seat and just kept driving, taking cuts that I'd never been down before but I knew were headed somehow out through the hills to the caravan he'd killed himself in, and picking up a hitchhiker I was planning to fuck before I had even pulled into the gravel, because the simplest way to hurt Michael was to act like his mother, and show him that now he had done what he'd done, I could easily settle into her life, sink into her dress, put on her red shoes and get myself a man who'd make my nose bleed, my hips black, my heart too blurred to see straight back into the past.

I swallowed some of the food the old lady had left me and lay in the caravan trying to come round, clean up. But I had trouble. That caravan was as good as a darkroom. And the images were cleaner then, so distinct they moved along my skin and through my insides. There were images of Michael that would not leave me, unlike the real thing. He met me at a service station where I was pumping gas, and he had just pulled his wagon in from the nearby beach he'd been surfing at. He only had boardies on, crusted with sand, knotted with a shoelace where the hair spiralled down on his belly. He'd cut his leg on the fin of his board and it was bleeding. He limped off to wash it at the tap on the concrete blocks at the end of the pumps. But he turned to stare back at me while he did it, looking hard at me while blood diluted under the long rub of his hand, streaked down his foot and dripped from it, joining the slick of petrol that belched from his car when it reached full. I didn't know then how precious that was, that stare.

I didn't know then how his usual look was past you, into the space beyond the left side of your head, as if your angel, your double, stood there, a trace of a past self that hung around or a future one, a shadow you hadn't quite stepped into. When he came closer, the day we met, I said, *I'm so sorry*, for spilling the gas, and he looked right at me, right in the face for a while, before his gaze slid away to the side, where I would learn it would mostly stay in our years together, eerie, cute, off-putting. It was long enough for so much damage to be done: in a single look I'd already learned him, especially the eyes with their troubles and stains and translucence rippling ring through ring, the pillar of bone up the middle of his chest, the thinned blood still drizzling down his ankle, the bud of joint there very white amidst the dark hair wrinkled darker with water. *Forget it*: those were the first words he said to me. I kept saying sorry. *No way, forget it*, he kept repeating. He wore a necklace like a dog-tag on his chest and on its bright metal there was still a single suspended fleck of the sea. He went on saying, *Hey forget it*, I went on staring at that drop, that clarity. I should have known then that Michael had brought me a terrible gift, of images that wouldn't leave.

In the caravan I thought, if I choose to follow Michael, that fleck of salt water glinting from his necklace might be the last thing I see.

But I also lay and thought about that water, that tiny circle shining and irrelevant . . . and thought I saw everything reflected in it. So much beauty left behind in something so useless. A nothingness and a shrine, at once, a waste and a universe. Like the cell he may have left behind in me.

I couldn't stay in the caravan thinking that. To think it was to watch all the questions, everything beginning with *if*, coming into focus like the ghost of Michael's fingers brushing words onto the glass for me. Waiting for my breath.

I crashed out of the caravan so hard I startled the old woman, who was in the garden. She was pushing a spinning blade on a stick along the concrete rim of the flower beds. It droned and squeaked, opened a dark scar of dirt. Her mouth opened in a smile as dark and dry.

I said nothing, because I couldn't. I walked straight ahead, through the weeds she had neatly stacked onto polythene, through loops of her washing, the wilted singlets as thin as webs strung across the light, not clothing but apparitions of thread. She clucked but she didn't bother staring at me. I heard the whining of her garden tool go on, the gritty sound of it chipping at the concrete.

I got to the beach and stayed there a long time. There weren't many people down there: a couple of grommets wagging school to surf, a few brisk pastel-toned women in plastic sun visors with handbag-sized dogs. A guy clicked by in jandals and a cap, a red-brown paunch jogging over his speedos and a cigarette pack tucked down above his arse. He stared at me through wraparound shades and slid his tongue in and out so I heard saliva jostling. But when I ignored him he just shrugged and squeaked past. Out to sea the light was so thick that it looked like someone had spilled sand along the horizon, and a triangle of shimmers too painful to focus on poured down. The waves moved in, like a diagram of themselves, measured and rustling. I thought about tipping Michael in with them, but every time I looked, black tangles of debris were dragged to the same place in each wave, as if the sea kept spitting up the same junk, unable to leave it. So I lay down then and closed my eyes, and the sound of the waves became a dream, the sound of Michael trying to fix his second-hand finds, taping their pages at one place while their spines just cracked straight open at the next one, until he gave up and plucked them, pinned them up round the flat. And we'd lie there on the bed under those strings of thinking and watch them, flicking yellow kites, and I'd forget how flimsy, how limited those theories seemed mingling on our wall when Michael climbed onto me and peeled my pelvis and his out of the basics of underwear and joined us, gently and wetly, into the one glazed body that we were meant to share.

When I woke I thought about fucking the hitchhiker there on the same stretch of beach. Stumbling the dunes, the hitchhiker had tried to talk, to add a dimension to the screwing, but once we reached the hard sand I'd pulled up my skirt and taken his fingers and shoved them under fabric, wedged them as far as I could get them in one jolt into me. As earnest as he was, he had gasped and unbuttoned. But he wasn't happy without his ideals for long. When we were done he went on talking, about himself when he found he couldn't learn about me. He told me about his project back at art school, an installation, cross-referencing cyberspace and God, he said. He blended things like chatroom threads with religious texts; he was going to call it Cannot Find Server. He was hitching this way to look through junk shops and dumps: he wanted old circuit boards, valves and cylinders, anything that looked mechanical, yet obsolete. He was going for a look of intricate components, technological complexity, yet ultimate emptiness, a vast systemic void. He was planning to splice other objects in, odd defunct icons from routine existence, and an active current would run through to randomly light up words he had taken from the Bible or the net: No New Messages, Unable to Establish a Connection, Click Here for a List of Errors. I told him I could give him a great piece: I told him to come back to the car with me. I still don't know if I might have gone through with it. I heard my voice talking as if it was a voice on tape: put it under Deleted Items, I said. I got as far as unlocking the car, brushing under the seat for the canister. It spun and slithered away from my hands, but I got hold and turned and offered it to him. I wasn't sure if it was shame or pity in the hitchhiker's face, but it was not neutral. He twitched as he was talking, nothing but shocked platitudes. But I thought we were talking about the postmodern, I said. I held Michael out. I said, he didn't leave a reason. So it was like all of the things you just said, pointless, disconnected, drained of value, arbitrary. All of the fucking clever things you just said. An uncommitted suicide, I said. Ha, an uncommitted suicide.

When the hitchhiker left, it was what I wanted. I let myself into the caravan alone. I still had Michael in my hands, and the residue of the hitchhiker trickling inside me. If and when I had to face the baby as definite, at least I could pretend that its source was unclear, and a child that had potentially nothing to do with Michael would be easier to dispose of. But really, I knew that line of thought was irrelevant. I knew it all broke down to just us three: me in the caravan, Michael in his chrome, the possible baby cooped inside me. One dead, one alive, the third one somewhere in the middle, undecided.

Uncommitted. Perhaps Michael had not let himself know either, had not been certain, until the very end, which way his decision, or indecision, would go, where it would take him. Perhaps he had been keeping his secret the way I had been keeping mine, even from myself. Perhaps when he came here he did not drive the distance head on and fixed on his suicide, but only felt the suggestion of death wavering along the outskirts of the strange road, a wayside of hazy possibilities, hissing as lightly as the fenceline crosses or the ferns. Perhaps he could lie down in the caravan and trick himself, dozily, pill by sip. Perhaps no capsule or gulp seemed terminal, not even the small knife he steered down his forearm, docking it finally in the deep mess of his wrist. He only cut one: maybe he still was irresolute, playing at that slash, unfocused. Maybe he was fooling himself. The same way I could walk back there from the beach and trick myself that my body was empty, except for an accidental rivulet of no one special's sperm.

Any way you stared at it, that caravan looked like death's door. When I walked back towards it after my short crash on the beach, the sun was shooting off it in all directions. I suppose my eyes were done in with more than just glare, but at first I didn't see the old girl was still outside. Only then, as I got across the section, I spotted her and I could tell she wasn't herself, not picking or fussing or digging at anything, just kneeling, making little bursts of off-pitch, scrawny movement, trying to claw up, then swaying back as if the buffalo grass was too spongy for take-off.

We'd hardly spoken two words but the sight of her, withered like that, made me run.

Her breath was scratchy, so I made her sit back and stop clambering about for a moment. She was not an easy old bugger to boss, so I got down with her and propped her up from the back and told her off, gently. She snapped, 'Leave off will you.' But after another lurch or two, she came back against me. Fragile lengths of rib shimmered through her old frock as she wheezed, and I could feel her heartbeat, puckering oddly. I didn't have to bully her still any more, so we just crouched, watching the caravan.

Finally, when her torso was steadier, she tampered with

the fingers I was holding her with and said, 'Well, that was a bad business.'

'What? D'you fall?'

'No,' she said, gruffly. 'I meant what your fella did. That was a bad business. What he came here and went and done to himself.'

I owed her something in reply but the cold in my lungs was packed solid. No words were getting in or out.

She said, 'Thought you'd keep mum about it, did you? I spotted you right away. It's a giveaway, your face, did you know that, dearie? I was wondering when you were going to pipe up and say. Anyway, I don't get that much call for the caravan. I only pin up that little note to rent it at the dairy and it's not like we get lots of outsiders through there. And never back-to-back like the two of you've been. We're the black stump out here, love. God's last shovelful.'

She nodded at the caravan, light still sharp all over that hutch. It looked even more rancid, bent on its piles, and the scruffy grass that I'd flicked full of smoke butts.

'We lived in that, you know. Me and Bert, when we first came here. He built the house later. Every last brick, he did. His back was a swine of a thing ever since.' She chuckled. 'I've never let it get run down to this state. Not in a month of blessed Sundays. But since your young man put his lights out in there I've felt too funny to get in and do it. The young cop gave it the once over for me, but you know young blokes. So I bring the bucket and things out to get stuck in and give it a real good going over. But I come over all unnecessary, I don't mind saying. And that's not something I'm used to, my girl.

'Not me,' she tutted on. 'Not ruddy likely. Tough as an old boot. Always have been. I tell myself, there's worse things happen to old birds like you stuck on their own. There was one not so long ago. Bludgeoned, she was, in her bed, and the fella they caught for it was only a mite. So I'm a darn sight luckier than that poor duck. Nothing to stop your young fella being one of those. And how would I've known.' She shifted, creakily, fastening herself, tapping away at sticking grasses. Her fingers were fibrous, a pinched blue at the joints. 'I need to get into gear now,' she said.

I stayed behind her, levering. I didn't have to see her eyes from there. We took a few steps once we were upright, but they were curtailed, doddery. I told her I could taxi her to the doctor's. Mad, her eyes were wide in their crinkle of skin and she looked like she fancied cuffing me.

'Not ruddy likely,' she said. 'I'll be right as rain. The way that doctor fluffs about gets me peeved. Good and proper.'

I hobbled her over to the house, her twitching me away, then relapsing, vexed, into my grip. In the long run she wasn't going to be thwarted. She waved me down a side of the house I hadn't been. Along the end wall were the remains of some kind of knocked-up cage or sun porch, just a frame stretched with tatters of black mesh.

I said, 'Michael had . . . a rotten time. When he was a kid.'

'Well,' she said. 'You hear a lot of that talk these days.'

'But Michael never would talk about it. He wouldn't tell me anything. Not any details. But once I had to drive his mother to the hospital and she jabbered out a whole load of stuff. I think she was sorry for a flash, but really only for herself. Anyway, she told me that once a guy she'd moved in with had lived at an old zoo park. He was closing it down, and he'd sold off most of the animals, and just had the leftover birds hanging round. He'd open the cages from time to time, but they couldn't get the picture. You know what they say, the cliché, too used to being locked up. So one night, when

Michael does something, or nothing, like little kids do, to piss this guy off, he drags him out and chucks him into one of those cages. She said some of the birds went crazy, him being in there, screaming like you can imagine. But it was the dead ones that bothered him the most. There were some that were dying cos the guy couldn't be bothered feeding them.'

'Sounds like a nasty piece of work.'

'She had a stack of them. His mother.'

She said, 'Well, I expected something like that when I never heard from the family. You'd think that someone'd be out to ask me about it, if he'd come from a decent bunch.'

'He didn't.'

'As things go, dear, you seem decent enough.'

I watched her from a pace behind, as she shuffled to the back door, holding back the streaks of vinyl that flagged away the flies. She jimmied off her boots and worked her feet into wizened velvet slippers. Holes were sawed into the tips to leave room for her corns.

She turned and said, 'If you ask me, mothers like that want being taken out and whipped. I can't fathom them. I would've gone to any length, for a kiddie. But Bert and me were never blessed. Not for want of trying mind you. That's why Bert started work on the house, y'know, even though we only had the dough to get going slowly, to put it up brick by brick. He said it'd come to him that while we were stopping in the caravan a little soul would think we didn't have the room to take it in. It sounds like an odd idea for a man to get, but it turned out that it really worried him. He couldn't rest easy in the old crate fretting that our little chap might be out there, in the ether or I-don't-know-where, looking down on us but feeling we weren't making the space to squeeze it in.'

There was a silence.

'I'm sorry,' I said finally. 'About it all. You having to find him. I don't know what . . . else to tell you. Do you need me?'

'I'll be right as rain. Like I said. You get used to being alone. I don't think I could stomach anyone now. Couldn't put up with it.'

I didn't think I should walk off but she clutched at the doorframe, wiry, not to be crossed.

As I moved back the cat sidled towards her, croaking. She nudged a saucer speckled with congealed meat towards it, talking back to it in coarse little yowls.

'Oh and this is Widow,' she said across the lawn towards me. 'When I was telling one of my pals down at the cardio club, she thought I said Pussy Widow, not Pussy Willow, you see. Silly old duffer. Then Widow just stuck. Just thought I'd tell you in case she tries to take over that caravan.'

'Widow,' I repeated.

'Still, I don't suppose you'll be long in staying. I imagine you've got plenty of things to be getting on with. Being alone'll do me. But it's hardly the ticket for a girl like you.'

I thought about my plenty as I wandered back to the caravan, lay down in its hovel.

There had been a baby there on the day of Michael's funeral. Someone tacked on to the 'family' through one of his 'uncles' had come along with one, humping it late along the aisle against her leather skirt, smirched with reflux. She'd slumped down beside me, yanking an older child into the pew before her. The older girl came down clumsily: there was a hard-backed Bible on the seat and she gripped her leg, tittering. All through the service I could hear mucus and misery squealing through the baby's tiny face. The mother stuck it out on one knee, shook it back and forth a while, making its whine come up in waves. When she tried to swing it to her other knee for a break it bucked and made a grab for her, catching the ring in her eyebrow. The ring unclipped and dangled from the socket, joined by a tiny dash of blood. Cursing, she shoved the baby sideways onto the girl's lap and stomped off down the carpet. But the girl only smiled, hauled the baby up by the armpits, and shimmied her ponytail down at it with jolts of her head. She nuzzled close, letting it suck on the baubles. In its dirty stretch-and-grow the baby's legs hung like little pipes.

Later, in the toilets, I was in a stall when I heard the mother laying the baby down on the tiles. Its stench choked the cubicle and it shrilled louder as she pushed its limbs in and out through its clothes. When I came out she had pulled paper down from the dispenser and was scratching at the dirty skin. She stuck the fresh nappy on wildly, then knelt back and stared, blankly, at the baby. It was still thrashing. She shot forward suddenly, dropping her face down right over the kid's. 'Am I pissing you off, am I? Well, now you fucking know how I feel,' she screamed at it.

'Go easy,' I said.

The mother looked at me. 'Oh yeah,' she said. 'Well, it's all yours if you want it.'

I said nothing.

'Nah, didn't fucking think so,' she said.

I walked away. Around the corner from the stalls was a long, bright bench of mirrors. Standing there was Michael's mother, eyelid hooked down by a little finger, calmly tracing the pink band with a tube of silver grit.

★

If there was one word I'd have expected to find appearing under my breath it was his brother's name. But if the caravan was death's door, death's windows didn't have a mark on them. I don't know why I kept looking. I kidded myself there might be some science to it, some principle of friction, the moisture content of exhalation, the differing qualities of light. I had no shortage of dreams of Michael's fingerprints, traced on the window, on my face, or on the inside of his flask. But no good ever came of them. Except the surplus of shivers which made me grope for his container and hunch around it, or snarl at it and shake it.

When I left the caravan I'd really no idea what to do. The old girl just shrugged when I dropped her keys back, as if she wasn't much bothered. But then she rambled beside me, out to the car, sinewy in a fresh frock. The cat toddled behind her at first, then darted off, shifty and primitive, flicking through the toetoe. When we got to the car, the old woman looked at the canister I had cradled in a jersey on the seat.

'You mind?' she asked me. I reached in and passed him into her hands.

'Well,' she said. She rocked him in her grip for a bit, weighing him. I think she was testing herself. I heard him in there, gliding along the surface.

'I got my Bert back in a ruddy box,' she said. 'Fancy that. Cardboard. I suppose it was daylight robbery for this.'

Then she said, 'He was a handsome type, your lad. Strapping, you know. I would have said robust. Not likely to go down without a fight. Still, it takes all sorts, I suppose.'

She bent down and tucked him into his nest in the car.

'Well,' she said. 'You want to come back for a spell, the caravan's there.'

I would have reached out and touched the ridges of her

cheek or knuckles, the streaks of scalp that shone through her hair, but she was too spry.

'Off you get now,' she grumbled.

I obeyed, and drove away, Michael taking the corners beside me.

From time to time as I drove I thought about making a switch, a trade, about driving straight to his mother's house and saying, Here, give me Smudge, I'll give you Michael. But I didn't feel like giving anything up.

On my last night in the caravan I had dreamt of upending his ash. But instead of his silt there was a rush of birds and pages, pulsing out into the dark, my breath pouring with them, a part of their luminous thrash. When I woke up I remembered the last message Michael had sent to me, a text before he left, just a dumb saying that I thought he tapped out for a joke: WHT DSN'T KLL U MKS U STRNGR. Sometimes at the point that you get a message, it makes no sense. What it means might get clearer, later, or you just have to breathe the meaning in for yourself. So I drove back to the city, choosing a vowel.

## Proudly sponsored by:

---

nielsen

Paperplus

David Bateman

DAVID LING

publishme.co.nz

RANDOM HOUSE
NEW ZEALAND

NEW ZEALAND

HarperCollins*Publishers*

STEELE ROBERTS

HYNDMAN
PUBLISHING

Sunday Star*Times

Victoria University Press

Whitcoulls

COMMUNITY POLYTECHNIC